I0586678

DANCING BUTTERFLY

DEBRA PARMLEY

PRAISE FOR DEBRA PARMLEY

Praise for *Dancing Butterfly* -

These flapper stories are wonderful and give us another glimpse into that time. Written so that you are transported back to that time by the descriptive writing and conversations. I could picture in my head how they were dressed and talked. Wonderful, interesting characters. With a blend of wit and charm, Debra Parmley is a modern-day Jane Austen.

— - COMFY CHAIR BOOKS

Praise for *Trapping the Butterfly* -

I couldn't put down until the end...a recommended read.

— - THE COLOR OF INK

An incredibly poignant story about a young girl exiting her cocoon and finding her strength! Beth's transformation from a meek girl forced to endure tyranny into a daring young woman was beautiful to see. The backdrop of jazz music, the prohibition and gangsters is exciting enough for a reader to imagine an inviting, sensual film unfolding in from of them.

— - MIMI SMITH - IND'TALE MAGAZINE

Start with a resort location, throw in a famous gangster with a detective hot on his trail, add a Jazz age setting, and you've got the makings for a fun read. Trapping the Butterfly has that and more, taking the reader on a Roaring Twenties tour through Hot Springs, Arkansas where the rich and famous traveled to "take the cure." ...The author ... describes what the spa treatments were like ... shows how life was changing in America, especially for young women... charming Jazz age story.

— - LONG AND SHORT REVIEWS

To all the women who long to dance, and can't because of circumstances.
To all the women who long to break free from circumstances.
May you soon be free.

CHAPTER 1

CHICAGO, ILLINOIS

March 1925

"Shimmy hard enough and nothing will hurt you."
- Suki

he band skipped a beat the moment Al Capone walked into The Green Mill. Flanked on the right and left by two large men in suits, with winter overcoats folded over their arms and wearing fedoras, he moved toward his favorite seat in the booth across from the side door on Lawrence Street; at the end of the bar where he could see both doors and everyone entering and leaving.

The bandleader immediately set the band to playing "Rhapsody in Blue," Al's favorite song. At that moment, the girls behind the curtain knew without looking, that Al Capone was in the house.

Suki bit her lip as she surveyed the crowded, smoky room.

He's here again, tonight. Walking in with Al. One of Al's men.

The handsome, hard-boiled man with the dark hair and intense brown eyes who'd been watching her every week for the past month, making her wonder if she was one of his fantasies, was back.

She was used to being a man's fantasy. It came with being a dancer. But it didn't mean they knew her. It didn't mean they saw beyond the showgirl on the stage.

Suki swallowed and touched her dangling right earring, a nervous habit, which brought her luck each time she danced.

A parting gift from her latest "uncle" on her sixteenth birthday, the silver and diamond earrings had become her good luck charms up to and until the time she'd moved out of her mother's house.

Tired of the revolving door of "uncles", she'd wanted to get away from them and to get out on with her own.

She'd changed her luck back then by working hard, being at the right place at the right time, and meeting the right people.

Maybe her luck would be even better tonight

and the handsome man who'd walked in with Al would ask to buy her a drink.

The handsome man liked watching her. She knew that much.

Low lighting and lowered voices filled the room where men in dark suits leaned toward each other, making private deals. With Al in the house, the energy of the room held a serious and high-spirited tone.

Gregarious and generous, Al lit up the room if he was in a good mood, as he was tonight. He waved to the bartender, who nodded back to him, and both of his men. "Frank. Joe."

"Hey, Tony," the man on Al's right side replied as he peeled away from Al. He took a seat at the end of the bar nearest the front door.

He wasn't the one Suki liked. She didn't know if he was Joe or Frank, but she wasn't interested in him.

The man had chosen his seat to help keep an eye on the front door, but the busty redhead who brought him a drink right away also might have had something to do with where he sat.

The energy changed as if the notes of "Rhapsody in Blue" spread into every corner of the building, bringing everything alive.

The song washed over Suki and she closed her eyes.

Got to have your game on to work here, but it's safer than out there, once you know the players and what to expect from them. Tips will flow tonight now that Al's here. Good.

More than good. This is a lifesaver.

She was out of scratch and her half of the rent was due in three days. Her thoughts turned from the blue of the song, to green.

Green, green, green.

Green spinach, lettuce, scratch, cash. Oh, that good, good green scratch.

I just need enough to make rent.

Jack McGurn's laugh made her eyes fly open. It didn't do to close them when he was near.

Making rent was just one of her worries. With a fine-tuned sense of listening developed from her childhood, she listened to the tones and nuances of Mr. McGurn's voice. Then she released a deep breath.

Jack McGurn, part owner of The Green Mill and one of Al's men, would be in a good mood tonight as long as no one screwed up.

Annie leaned close to whisper into Suki's ear, startling her. "His name is Frank."

"Who?" Suki pretended she didn't know who Annie was talking about.

Annie rolled her eyes. "That guy you're watchin'. The one who's been watchin' you."

There was no point denying it.

"Thanks, Annie."

"No problem, doll." Annie moved away to fuss

with a shiny silver-sequined hairpiece atop her bobbed red hair.

Now that Al's song had ended, Suki's dance music began to play.

She moved onto the stage, gliding into her first position, which always brought cheers from the crowd.

Suki was one of their new favorite hoofers. The dance move was just innocent enough and cheeky enough to make a man smile back at her, as her white, beaded chemise dress caught the light.

Tonight her dance costume and role was of an innocent, a good girl role she'd play briefly because Emily was still out sick.

Though word was Emily might've left town after Mr. McGurn had grown angry with her boyfriend and, by association, her.

Emily's boyfriend, the jazz singer Boots Malloy, hadn't been seen in a few days either. He'd taken a new job at a rival club, and Jack McGurn didn't tolerate betrayals.

Whatever had happened, Suki was staying out of it, not asking questions. She'd spent as little time at the club as possible the past two weeks to avoid Mr. McGurn and his foul mood. Though she couldn't help wondering about Emily.

Wonder what she got herself into. Something. Because something's off about her disappearing.

Emily isn't as innocent as she appears. But everyone

always wants to help sweet, innocent Emily. Even Mr. McGurn, lately. That could've turned out bad for her. He could be ruthless. Hope she's okay.

Emily had the sweet, round face of a cherub with curly blonde hair. Mr. McGurn needed a blonde, a redhead, and a dark-haired girl, in that order, for the club's dancers.

A dancer to fit every man's fantasy. Though McGurn employed more than just three dancers.

Suki, Emily's complete opposite with dark hair, pale skin, and blue eyes, was far from innocent. She'd seen and experienced the rough side of life at a young age. But she could play at being an innocent for the show.

Her experiences had taught her to keep away from men like Mr. McGurn. Had taught her ways to stay safe and not to depend on a man the way her mother had.

Suki was an independent dancer, with her own apartment and a roommate.

She always paid her own way.

Her thoughts turned to McGurn and how his mood had changed lately.

Now Emily isn't here to attract him. If he'd wanted Emily and did something to Boots and then Emily had said no... anything could've happened.

None of the dancers are talking about it. I'd best not ask.

Mr. McGurn preferred blondes and was known

as an incurable skirt chaser, chasing every blonde around him.

It was no coincidence most of the girls he hired were blonde. Normally he paid little attention to Suki. And yet, when she'd come into work tonight, he'd said, "Don't make plans tonight, doll. Stick around. You're joining me for drinks after the show."

It wasn't a request.

It was also hard to get off her mind, as she had no desire to take a turn on McGurn's casting couch.

He hadn't bothered to ask if she had plans tonight. Just ordered her not to have any.

Frank had escorted Al to his seat, and then moved toward the bar.

She noted the powerful way he moved. She'd much rather be having drinks with Frank tonight.

As her body moved through her dance routine she finally lost herself in the music and the dance, forgetting everything else.

With dance, she could shimmy hard and forget the past. Within the dance, she was free.

Shimmy hard enough and nothing will hurt you.

With that favorite phrase in her head again she was halfway through her last number, giving the innocent role her all. Just at the point where she moved from a cheeky look, out over her shoulder to the audience as her body faced away from them, and then led into a spin to face toward them again, her left earring flew off onto the dance floor.

Breaking a performance rule, she glanced down.

Oh, no. My lucky earring...

Horrified, she watched as the earring hit the wooden floor, only to be immediately kicked by a woman crossing the floor from one table to another, spinning it over to a heavy man who'd just pushed his chair back to stand, and then to a thin flapper who'd gotten up to dance.

For a terrifying few seconds, she'd thought the heavy man might step on the earring and smash it completely, but then the flapper who'd gotten up to dance kicked it again and it skidded to stop.

Right at Frank's feet as he stood near the end of the bar, closest to the stage.

He bent down and picked it up, palming it in his hand.

Breathing in relief that the earring hadn't been lost or damaged, Suki moved through the rest of her dance routine, knowing she could collect it from him after her set when the next hoofer came on.

FRANK HAD BEEN WATCHING the showgirl named Suki for weeks.

With her pale skin and dark hair the dish was a study in contrasts, her blue eyes always alert and lively. Her short straight hair flipped and swung when she turned her head a certain way and she knew it. The cut emphasized the pale skin of her jaw and her slender neck. She had hoofer's legs, toned from dancing, and pale skin; the fringe on her short white dress swung with her movements, showing them off. Trim, delicate ankles and slim feet moved rapidly as she danced in white beaded heels.

She looked at him directly, caught him watching her, and held his gaze. That was one of the things he liked about her.

Suki had spunk, and she didn't take any guff from any of the men in the club either. Though she knew when to be quiet, she was no pushover.

He liked a woman with spunk.

Fire in the eyes meant fire in the bedroom.

His last girlfriend, Bernice, had the passion of a cold cup of coffee. Sure, there was caffeine to keep you going like you'd find in any cup of java, but it neither tasted good nor warmed a man.

Suki could warm a man from the stage with just one look.

Those eyes... blue come and stroke me, eyes.

He was more than drawn to her even as he sized up the room tonight, doing his job. Everything was as it should be, so he could watch her now.

When her earring flew off and skidded across the floor to eventually stop at his feet, he bent to pick it up with satisfaction.

The earring was important to her; he'd seen that while watching her expressions change as the earring had been passed around the floor like a hockey puck. He'd seen how relieved she was that it was safe.

Holding the delicate jewelry in his palm, he watched her dance.

Good. She'd be coming for the earring now palmed in his hand. He'd positioned himself at the end of the bar where he could see the entrance, as watching the entrances and exits were part of his job. But he'd still be near the hidden stairs behind the bar, which led to the green room for entertainers as well as the private rooms below.

She'd have to walk past him to go downstairs to the green room where her coat and hat would be, if she planned to leave after her set.

Finishing her set, Suki gave a little bow to her applause; she then thanked the jazz band players, and then moved out of the limelight so the next hoofer could go on.

He watched her walk toward him across the floor; those toned dancer's legs moving smoothly, her dark hair and the fringe on her white dress swinging as her blue eyes met his and held.

Not breaking that gaze, he gazed right back and she barely blinked.

This was no shy dancer, and she was headed straight for what she wanted. Which was the earring in his palm.

He'd like to see her heading toward him wanting

something else. He'd be more than happy to give it to her.

Then she was standing in front of him, cool and breathy. Not afraid. Not shy.

"We haven't been introduced." Her words came out fast and low.

He leaned closer to hear her. "No, we haven't," he said.

"I'm Suki."

"Nice to meet ya, Suki." He said her name slowly and watched her reaction.

There was a glimmer of something in her eyes. Attraction.

He knew how to read the signs. "Frank Omato." He reached for her hand, the soft, pale skin of her hand now in his. He kissed the back, watching the color in her cheeks rise.

So, she liked that.

"Nice to meet you, Frank."

"Suki, short for Susan?" Frank asked.

"Yes." She nodded. "Susan Chesterfield."

He didn't comment on the last name and kept his eyes from glancing down to her breasts, bare beneath her heavily beaded white dress.

Instead he focused on her eyes, avoiding her red lips and the way they'd parted as she breathed out to answer him.

"You prefer Ski?" he asked.

She nodded. "Yes."

~

FRANK'S VOICE was doing something to her, something she'd never felt before, as his tones reached deep down inside. Her body responded to those tones, making her want to lean in closer. Softening her approach to him. Making her want to touch him.

The moment Frank took her hand and his hand touched hers, she felt a connection, stronger than the typical, oh you look good, attraction she usually had with good-looking men.

Her skin warmed beneath his and she felt the connection all the way up her arm.

Then Frank kissed the back of her hand and goose bumps pebbled across her shoulders and neck.

This is one of those once-in-a-lifetime things, this connection.

She didn't know how she knew, but she did.

He asked for her real name and she gave it.

"Susan Chesterfield." Heat rose in her cheeks as she blushed, something she hadn't done since she was thirteen and Johnny Scarlatti teased her on the playground.

And that was what Johnny had teased her about so long ago. Her budding breasts, which all the boys had noticed, while her mother was too busy drinking and entertaining the next "uncle", who always noticed them.

Her mother stayed too busy pleasing the latest man, too busy to buy Suki proper undergarments or to teach her anything about being a woman, or sex.

Suki had learned about sex all on her own. By being observant and, later, with the help of one of those "uncles" who noticed everything and knew how to do everything. She'd learned how to please a man and lost any shyness she'd ever had.

Tonight, this was a whole different kind of blush, for she wasn't shy.

Frank was a gentleman treating her like a lady, while her body warmed from being so near to him.

The show dress didn't hide her bare breasts and she wore nothing but silk stockings and silk panties underneath.

She was fairly certain he'd noticed, though he'd been gentleman enough not to look at her chest.

He turned her palm over, creating more delicate shock waves along her body at his touch.

"I have something of yours," he said.

"Yes," she breathed as the chemistry arced between them like an electrical storm she'd once watched, the light show crackling across the treetops.

Frank was a strong and dangerous man, an enforcer in Al's gang. This attraction between them, like an electrical storm, was dangerous to play with and impossible to ignore.

Just like Frank Omato.

He placed the earring in her hand, and then with a light caress of her palm pulled his fingers away, making her catch her breath.

She glanced down at the earring. "Thank you."

"You're welcome." He closed her fingers back around the earring and then released her hand again.

She felt the loss of his touch, and stepped back, her gaze flying back up to meet his. She wanted him to touch her again and knew he'd read that in her eyes.

"Dinner after," he asked with such assurance it almost wasn't a question. "If you're free tonight."

"Yes," she breathed again, almost a whisper. "I'll have dinner with you."

Suddenly he turned his gaze away from her with a frown as his full attention focused on something near the front door.

She glanced there, too, wondering what was important enough to break the intimate connection forming between them.

His right hand moved swiftly toward his heart, beneath his jacket, at the same time as his left hand wrapped firm around her left arm, moving her behind him.

He stepped forward, in front of her, to shoot. "Go," he said. "Get downstairs!"

Crouching down behind him she moved behind the bar, where Tony, the bartender, had crouched down, holding the door in the floor behind the bar open for everyone to escape.

"Come on, hurry!" Tony said.

FRANK, positioned at the end of the bar farthest from the front door to watch for trouble, had angled himself so that Suki was right in front of him. He could still see in his peripheral vision past her to the left, to where his boss Al sat, and to the right to watch the front half of the club.

Joe was there, but he was really supposed to watch the door more than the rest of the club.

Occasionally Frank would scan the whole club, but all was well, and he was giving Suki as much of his full attention as his job allowed.

He looked into her pretty blue eyes and noted every nuance of her mood.

This dame knew what she wanted, and she wanted him.

Dinner was a sure bet, and odds were high on the after-dinner entertainment, with this pretty dancer.

She was saying yes, she'd have dinner with him,

when movement and noise in the front of the club caught his attention.

"Hey wait!" The doorman raised his voice at a few men who'd stepped inside the club, still wearing their overcoats. "You got to come back and check in at the door."

Everyone had to remove their coat before entering, to have it checked for big guns.

Jack McGurn took no chances in his club, and tonight was Al's night to be in the club.

These guys should've been stopped long before they were inside.

Joe had been laughing with a busty redhead about something and should've been up and over to stop the men, if they went past the doorman.

The man in front of the trio of outsiders turned back toward the doorman as if to answer, but then spun back around whipping a Tommy gun from beneath his overcoat and raising it to start spraying.

His first shots ripped into Joe, and his two partners behind him drew more weapons.

Frank quickly reached for his 1911 beneath his suit jacket. At the same time, he moved Suki behind him. "Go," he said. "Get downstairs!"

He stepped in front of her, blocking her with his body as he pulled his gun up to shoot.

Aiming the .45-caliber pistol he took a shot at the first assailant, hitting him straight between the eyes as the other two moved into the club, guns roaring.

Frank's one shot took the man down instantly, even as other shots by the rest of Al's gang hit him on the way down. Frank never wasted time.

He took the first shot and immediately searched for the next target.

Known for his dead shots, Frank had a well-earned reputation.

He didn't like wasting ammunition.

Though he practiced every week with the rest of Al's gang, even if he hadn't, his aim had always been good, and he had a good eye.

Frank was a natural-born shooter, from the time he was a boy, and within Al's gang was the best of any of them with a Tommy gun.

A gun he wished he had now.

As if he'd guessed that wish, Tony slid Frank a Tommy gun from behind the bar.

Frank's right hand slipped his 1911 back into his shoulder holster as his left hand crossed his body, stopping the submachine gun from falling off the edge of the bar.

If the first guy had had better aim, Frank could've been an unlucky stiff.

But the first guy was no expert with a Tommy gun.

It appeared the man hadn't used one much, and his aim had only been spraying and praying.

17

SUKI DUCKED down as the first gunshots overhead exploded bar glasses and the mirror behind the bar, showering her and Tony with broken slivers while women screamed, the repeating *rata tat tat* of the Thompson submachine guns punctuating the women's screams.

Everything was happening so fast and loud, she wanted to hide and cover her ears.

The noise was deafening with the roar of the "Tommy guns" and the screams of the women. She couldn't hear what Tony was shouting at her.

She shook her head at him showing she didn't understand.

"Go through the tunnels!" he shouted.

"I've never been!" she shouted back. "How do I get out?"

Tony put his head down as glass shattered above him, and then he looked at her again. "Follow one of the men. Go! Go on! Blow!"

She ran down the steps toward safety.

Hurrying, her right fist holding the earring and pushing off the wall next to her, she was almost to the bottom when she stepped out with her right foot off of two steps as if it were one, and fell onto the concrete.

Landing on the outer side of her foot as it rolled under, she fell hard onto the bone of her ankle, which cracked, sending a shock wave of pain from her foot all the way up her leg, past her knee.

She cried out, her arms reaching to catch herself as she fell, but still she was falling. Her clenched fist failed to help her stop and she landed on her forearm, the wind knocked out of her and pandemonium raining down from upstairs.

Footsteps were hurrying down behind her, but she didn't look to see who it was.

She pulled herself off to the side, where whomever it was who was in a hurry wouldn't trip over her.

Men from the private gambling rooms near the tunnel had run out of the rooms, opening the doors which led to the tunnels and their getaways as Chicago lightning tore up the club upstairs.

The gunshots were only slightly muffled down here, and the panic was still fresh with everyone.

She could see six men running down the tunnel and around the corner, moving fast.

Everything was moving and happening much too fast.

Mr. McGurn's voice behind her said, "Suki what're you doing? Get up."

She tried to rise but couldn't put weight on her foot as pain spread up her ankle and leg again.

She fell back down on the floor, wondering how she'd get away. Starting to panic, she looked up. "I can't."

Then Al's voice boomed out behind McGurn, louder than the gunshots. "She clipped?"

"I don't know," McGurn answered.

Suki looked up at Al and then realized her lip was bleeding.

Al looked right at her, frowning. "Tell Frank about the dame. Get her outta here."

"I'll handle it," Lou, the third man said, and ran back up the stairs towards the gunfire.

"You don't say a word to the cops," Mr. McGurn said to her. "You don't know from nothing."

"I'm a clam." She placed her finger on her lips, ignoring her bleeding lip to emphasize her silence, and then the men hurried on past her, their job to guard Al Capone.

McGurn led the way, Al behind him and, two men following Al, they sped away into the tunnel.

To McGurn, she was just a dancer.

Replaceable within a day.

He was mad, probably because she'd been in the way of their escape. One more thing for him to have to deal with. One more thing wrong in his club.

Can't believe he said that to me. As if I'd breathe a word to the cops about anything the men did.

I'd have to be a fool to do that and I've never been a fool.

She brought her finger away and saw the blood on it.

At least Mr. Capone had asked if I'd been hit. He had no time to stop, of course, but at least he'd shown brief concern.

Mr. McGurn didn't give a damn.

He never even asked if I'd been shot, even after Al asked him. He didn't care, as long as I wasn't a problem for him. That's all he cares about.

Touching her lip again she felt a small sliver of glass.

Pulling the glass loose, she dropped it to the floor and rose on her hands and knees to head for the green room, crawling, still holding her earring in her hand, but hurrying as fast as she could.

There were still gunshots upstairs, but they were slower, like a car running out of gas.

Inside the green room, she sat up and put her lucky earring back on. Pulling her white beaded headpiece off, she then shook her head and moved her fingers through her short black hair, to shake other slivers of glass out.

For a moment, she glanced up at her coat hanging from a rusted hook in the wall, along with her red cloche hat.

Too high to reach without standing.

She tried to stand again with no luck. It only made the throbbing worse.

Deciding to abandon them, she crawled quickly out of the green room, and toward the tunnel.

Outside the green room she paused.

She could hardly crawl away down those tunnels.

Her stockings were torn now, but her lip had stopped bleeding.

She had to find a way to get back up onto the street and get away from The Green Mill, but she'd never been in the tunnels they used in the early morning hours to deliver hooch all over the city and didn't know where this one led.

All she knew was she needed to follow them and get out of here.

She also needed a doctor to look at her foot.

Finally, there was a solid break in the shooting and footsteps pounded down the stairs.

"Suki, what are you doing on the floor? Get up."

He was there. *Frank.* Insisting she rise.

"You should've been gone when I told you to go. Come on, doll, and get up now. We've got to get outta here."

She tried to rise again on her feet, not answering him, as pain made tears run down her face, and she gasped.

"Baby, were you hit?" His voice now held concern for her; in a tender tone she'd never have guessed in such a commanding man.

Suki shook her head. "No, I don't think so."

He'd stepped in front of her, and she saw his shoes and his cuffed pant legs, before she looked up to where his arm was there, ready to help her up— his left hand helping her stand, while his right held a Tommy gun.

"Steady," he said. "I got you."

She looked up into his concerned brown eyes.

"I tried to run and fell on the stairs. Turned my ankle and landed hard. I can't walk on it by myself."

"No time to look at it. Come on, I'll get you outta here."

Frank would know where the tunnels went.

Frank was in tight with Al and, as a trusted enforcer, knew most of Al's business.

She'd trust him to get her out to safety. She nodded and tried to take a step onto her right foot.

Pain throbbed from her right ankle and she gasped again, sinking down, unable to catch her breath.

Deep brown eyes looked into hers as he caught her. "Steady."

He put one arm around her and helped her rise.

"Put your arm around me," his voice commanded as he held her up with one arm, while the other held his gun.

She slid her arm around him, bringing them closer.

It was clear she'd damaged her foot enough she couldn't walk on it alone.

But with Frank's help she could hobble and get away.

~

THE GREEN MILL WAS QUIET.

It was done. Over.

Frank surveyed the room.

All three assailants were dead.

The sudden silence assailed his ears, which still rang from the gunshots.

The chopper squad had made a mess of the room. Broken glass and mirrors littered everything and when he took a step, it crunched under his foot.

He ignored the blood and the men who'd been cut down.

Dead bodies didn't shock his senses any more.

They were dead, but he was alive and that was all that mattered.

Cops will be on the way if they aren't already.

Now he had to move and make sure everyone was out.

Lou had said a dancer was hurt and Al wanted her moved. Where is she? Must be downstairs.

Lou had come back up, delivered the message, and then gone back down the stairs with Tony.

Al's gang had cleared the building. Frank would be the last one out.

He took hold of the door behind the bar and made sure he closed it behind him as he went down the stairs.

The hidden door in the floor behind the bar was hard to see once closed. When the cops arrived, the club would be empty.

Frank moved quickly down the stairs and at the bottom he saw Suki sitting by the entrance to the tunnels, balled up and looking at him with those big blue eyes and blood on her lip.

He frowned.

Why didn't she listen and go when I told her to?

Seeing blood, he grew more concerned.

Had she been shot?

He moved quickly.

Got to get her out of the club.

"Suki, what are you doing on the floor? Get up. You should've been gone when I told you to go. Come on, doll, and get up now. We've got to get outta here."

She didn't answer him but attempted to get up. Tears ran down her face and she gasped.

Blood.

There was blood on her lip and splotches on her white dress.

Where was it coming from?

"Baby, were you hit?"

Suki shook her head. "No, I don't think so."

She might not know.

He stepped in front of her, trying to assess where she might've been hit.

It didn't appear she'd been shot. There wasn't enough blood.

Still, he didn't like to see her hurt and bleeding. He reached out to help her to stand.

"Steady," he said as he helped her up. "I got you."

She looked up into his eyes. "I tried to run and fell on the stairs. Turned my ankle and landed hard. I can't walk on it by myself."

"No time to look at it. Come on, I'll get you out of here."

She nodded and stepped onto her right foot. She gasped and sank down, but he held onto her with one arm.

"Steady." Placing an arm around her, he said, "Put your arm around me."

Her slim, soft arm slid around him. "Atta girl."

Clearly, she's hurt. Ankle twisted and sprained or broken. Gotta take her to the doc.

"Hold on," he said.

She held on tight as if she were frightened.

He tightened his arm around her.

I need to get her out before the cops come.

Somehow, even though they hadn't gone on a first date yet, he already felt protective. Something about her brought that out in him.

She needed him. And she felt good next to him as he put his arm around her and drew her closer.

They weren't safely away yet, but they would be and then he'd see that she was taken care of.

With a firm grip on her waist he helped her walk, hoping they'd get away before the cops got there.

Frank glanced over his shoulder and listened.

CHAPTER 2

"Get a wiggle on," Frank said.

"I'm doing my best," Suki said. "So far, so good. No cops. I hope I'm not slowing you down too much."

"Just keep moving," Frank said.

He moved Suki down the tunnels beneath the street, with him holding her close and her hobbling along. He knew where he was going and moved them as fast as he could, given her inability to walk on her own.

It took them much longer than Frank would've liked. The floor was broken and uneven in some places that needed repairs.

It was dark, even with the bare light bulbs hanging from the ceiling so they wouldn't run into a wall tunnel, but it wasn't easy or fast.

The bulbs were spaced far apart, leaving gaping

black holes between them. Fortunately, the black stretches of holes were almost always placed at corners, except for one long black hole where a bulb was burned out.

That section left them in the dark, moving by his senses and memory. He moved warily, aware the darkness could hide enemies.

Could be the bulb was burned out, or someone shot it out to prevent anyone from following.

The person who shot it out could still be waiting in the dark.

"Frank, this gives me the heebie jeebies," Suki said.

"Don't worry, babe, I got you." His arm tightened around her, keeping his thoughts to himself.

He wasn't afraid, just calm and watchful, the way he always got when there might be danger to him and his.

They reached the next block beneath the streets and turned the corner.

"I'm glad you know where you're going. I'm lost," Suki said.

"Never lost when you're with me," he said. "I know this town inside and out."

"And underneath."

He grunted, almost a laugh.

She smiled. "Where are you taking me?"

"This tunnel ends under the theater. Its basement has a hidden door. Once we get there, we'll look like a normal couple getting out for some air, or leaving the theater if there's been a show."

"A normal couple with guns," Suki said.

Frank grunted again. "Yeah. We'll see."

Finally, the tunnel ended.

Looking at her, Frank said, "Just act natural, like we've been out to the theater. If a copper stops us, that's what we tell him. Got it?"

"Got it." She looked at him, curious why they'd stopped and were just standing there. "What now?" she asked.

"Looking for a place to cheese it." He moved toward a wall where three barrels stood and placed the Tommy gun behind them.

"I wish you didn't have to go up there, unarmed," Suki said.

"Never unarmed, babe." He patted his shoulder holster and gun. "I have a permit for the 1911, but cops frown on carrying a machine gun in the street."

"Oh, yes. They would," Suki said.

Cautiously, Frank undid the latch that allowed a door to swing away from him, into an empty basement room.

After a pause, while he listened and watched, he and Suki stepped inside, and he closed the door behind them.

It was dead silent.

They were too far from the club to hear

anything, and they were still beneath the street, away from cars and people.

Suki breathed deeply, relaxing for the first time since Frank had pulled her behind him. "I like it here. It's quiet."

"I like it, too," Frank said.

They looked at each other, enjoying the moment.

Frank had both hands free now, and he wanted to touch her.

He reached out and touched her cut lip with his thumb, gently.

Her breath came out slow, with a sigh.

Just when he would have leaned in to kiss her, Suki's foot throbbed again, taking her breath, and she winced.

The moment was broken.

Frank caught her and took the weight off her hurt foot. "Come on. Let's get you some help."

Together they hobbled through the basement, until Frank opened the door and stopped at the foot of the stairs.

"Oh, horse feathers," Suki sighed, and her expression fell at the sight of the stairs.

She'd completely forgotten that having gone down a flight of stairs to get away, she'd soon have to go up a flight to continue until she got back up onto the street.

Frank grunted again, and then swept her up into his arms.

Suki gasped in surprise, but he was already two steps up the stairs before she thought to stop him.

"Frank." She placed her hand on his chest.

"Just enjoy the ride, sugar," Frank said.

And she did, relaxing her body next to his.

At the top of the stairs he gingerly set her down, and they resumed their slow dance to the front door.

They were in the lobby of a theater that was closed for the night. As they approached the entrance to the street, Frank fished around in his pocket for a set of keys.

Suki laughed. "What, you can break into buildings now?"

"Doll face, I'm breaking us out. We already broke in."

"True." She grinned and, eyeing all the keys, said, "Where'd you get all those keys?"

Frank grinned. "My boss knows a lot of people."

"Your boss knows everyone," she replied.

Finally, they were at the front door.

Frank unlocked it, and then cracked the door open to poke his head out, looking left then right.

As the cold Chicago wind blew past him, Suki gasped and shivered.

Hearing it, Frank ducked back inside and shrugged out of his jacket.

"What are you doing now?" she asked as she rubbed her arms.

"Giving you a blanket." Frank threw it around

her shoulders, and then opened the door to step outside, drawing Suki behind him.

On the street, away from the club and the noisy recent memory of gunfire and violence, she raised her head to look at their surroundings again and asked, "Where to now?"

His arm moved around her again. "My car is parked down the street. I'm taking you to see a doctor."

She gasped. "Are you sure it's safe for you to take me to a hospital?"

Gangsters covered with blood spatter and carrying guns usually avoided hospitals and police stations.

He was touched by her concern for him, but she had no real idea how things worked if she thought he was taking her to a hospital.

He laughed. "I'm not taking you to a hospital, doll."

"Okay," she answered, her voice quiet.

"I know a doc."

"You know a doc?"

"What are you, a magpie?" He gazed into her eyes. "Trust me to keep you safe and take care of you. I know where to take you."

"Okay, Frank. I'll trust you."

He nodded with approval on his face.

When she stumbled, he tightened his arm around her. "If we weren't on a public street I'd pick you up and carry you again, but I don't want to draw too much attention."

She liked the thought of Frank carrying her again. It led to thoughts of him carrying her into the bedroom.

Finally, they reached a black shiny car and he stopped, looking around. Then he opened the passenger door and helped her inside.

She placed her hand on his arm. "Thank you, Frank, for helping me to get away from there. I was behind the eight ball, and I don't need any trouble."

He looked down at into her thankful blue eyes. "My pleasure, doll." He closed the door and walked around to the driver's side.

He opened the door, sat down, then put his 1911 on the seat between them and glanced at her.

"Hope it doesn't make you nervous there." He nodded his head toward the gun.

She shook her head no.

Guns did make her nervous.

But it wasn't as if anyone was pointing it at her. And the men in the club always carried guns.

Clearly, by the way he was acting, Frank thought it necessary for the gun to be there, between them, where he could reach it fast.

He must be concerned about more gunmen coming after us.

The thought terrified her as she remembered the noise of the guns and the women screaming.

She sat quiet, remembering, and trying to ignore the pain in her foot.

Frank started the car and they rode in silence though the dark night, which allowed them both to process the events of the evening.

Everything had happened so fast there'd been no time for that until now.

Suki closed her eyes and tried to ignore the pain in her ankle shooting from her foot up her calf as they sped on into the night. She didn't open them until she felt the car slow down to turn.

Frank was pulling into a driveway in a quiet neighborhood with lots of trees.

The little white house appeared dark and closed until Frank eased the car along the gravel drive, which ran beside the house.

In the back of the house, one window shone a light onto the dark back lawn. The back door stood partly cracked and Suki could see lights inside and a man moving about.

"Stay put," Frank said as he parked the car.

She nodded at him.

He holstered his gun again, got out and closed the door, then walked to the back step and knocked on the doorframe.

"Hey, Doc." He spoke so quiet, Suki could only figure out his words from watching his mouth.

The doctor who met Frank at the door wore a white bloodstained apron and bloody gloves. He didn't open the door but held his hands up to show his gloves and then gestured to Frank to come in.

Frank shook his head and pointed to where Suki sat in the car.

The doctor said something, glanced at her, and then moved back inside to his patient.

Frank walked over to her door and opened it. "Taxi service," he said with a grin. Then he scooped her up into his arms to carry her inside.

It felt natural to slip her arms around his neck and to hold on. She breathed in his scent, wanting to close her eyes. If not for her throbbing ankle, she would have.

His arms seemed the only safe, strong, and steady place she'd find this dark and dangerous night. She clung to him.

He carried her through the back door.

"Set her down over there." The doctor shrugged with his shoulder toward a chair against the wall. "I'll be with you once I finish removing these bullets."

There was one operating table—a large dark-haired man, face down with his back to them, bleeding from a wound in his back, occupied it.

He'd turned his head to watch them as they came in.

Frank nodded to him.

The man winced as the doctor focused on removing a bullet.

A few seconds later the doctor said, "Aha," and held up a bullet, which he then dropped into a metal pan with a clunk. "Got it." Taking gauze, he then pressed it to the wound to stop the bleeding.

"Now, tell me what happened," He spoke to Suki, and focused on her for a brief a moment, in between bandaging his other patient.

"I was running down the stairs at the club tonight when I fell and turned my foot, landing on it wrong," she said. "It rolled under and I landed on my right ankle bone hard, onto the concrete."

"Can you walk on it?"

"Well, I tri—"

Frank cut her off. "No. She can't. She was crawling when I found her. She wouldn't have made it out if I hadn't helped her walk. She has no business trying to walk on it by herself." He spoke as if he were the authority on her and her injury.

"That remains to be seen, but see it we shall," the doctor said. "Once I finish here I'll look at it."

"Thank you," she said.

He looked at Frank. "This will take a while. Go in the other room if you'd like a little hair of the dog."

"Thanks, Doc. Lemme get Suki a drink first."

"Certainly. But I don't have wine or champagne for women, only hard liquor. I don't get many women here. Bring in the medicinal rum."

"I'll take anything if it makes this pain stop," she said.

"It will," the doctor said.

Frank stood and headed into the kitchen, toward the living room, as if he knew exactly where to go.

Suki watched him wearily as the events of the evening started to hit her hard now that the adrenaline had worn off.

Know where to go? Of course, he does. Frank knows a lot of things. He's that sort of man. The kind who gets things done.

Frank headed to the other room and then came back, carrying a bottle marked Chapin's Pure Old Rum bottled in bond under the supervision of the U.S. Government by The American Medicinal Spirits Company.

"Goodness," she said as she read the label. "Our government is bottling rum now? But nobody else can. What a racket."

"Yeah," the man on the other table said. "Ain't it, though? But they don't sell enough to hurt business. Only doctors can buy that brand. This ain't government hooch, though."

"So, it's not what's on the label?"

"It's better than what's on the label," Frank said.

He poured the rum into a clear glass and held it out to her. "Try it. If you like it, I'll make another one."

She reached for the glass and took a sip, avoiding the cut on her lower lip, which might sting if alcohol touched it. She let the liquor warm her mouth and then her throat as it slid down, warming her from the inside.

Different than other drinks she'd had, this one had spices she couldn't place. "What's in it?"

"It's spiced rum," Frank said. "Comes all the way from Jamaica."

"Mmm," she said. "Pretty good stuff. Strong, though."

"All the better for pain. Just keep sipping." He winked, which made her smile.

"Thank you." She smiled back at him.

"You're welcome."

"I hope this helps," she said. Her voice came out more nervous than she intended, so she took another swallow.

"It will," the doctor said over his shoulder, where he was working on the second bullet. "Give it a minute."

Soon the drink was starting to help; she felt warm and began to relax everywhere except her foot, which was still throbbing.

"I'll go make another," Frank said.

For good measure she sucked down another warm swallow of rum.

Her foot throbbing told her that another might not be enough to deaden the pain. She took a fourth swallow for even better measure.

She eyed the nearly empty glass and then raised it to her lips.

One more, for the best measure of all.

Frank came back into the room with his own glass.

"Yes, this is definitely helping," she said, holding up her glass. "Though my foot is still throbbing."

Frank nodded, his gaze steady on her face, his expression contemplative as he watched her.

She wondered what he was thinking as she took another swallow, leaving the glass empty.

With the way he was looking at her, she wasn't sure of anything except the heat rising within her, slowly moving up from deep in her belly, toward her chest, her heart. From the way it was spreading throughout her body it could overtake her, taking her anywhere.

She tried to think of something else.

The dance, her shoes, her dress, her stockings. The rain falling outside.

But all she could think of was Frank. His deep brown eyes looking at her. His mouth as he spoke. How it might feel if he kissed her with those lips. His broad shoulders and how tall and strong he was. How he made her feel small, but safe.

Taking her empty glass with one hand and setting it down, he lifted his other hand toward her face and stepped closer, though he'd only been inches away, until his body was next to hers.

His fingertips lightly brushed down the line of her jaw. Then, dipping his head to hers, his thumb curving beneath her chin, he softly guided her face up toward him as his lips descended.

His soft, warm lips coaxed hers, careful at first because of the cut and then coaxing with more pressure until she gave a small gasp, her mouth widening, allowing his tongue to press inside her mouth, still coaxing, and the pull toward him irresistible.

He tasted of rum, and the kiss, intoxicating as the liquor she'd been drinking, warmed her even more as she surrendered her mouth to his tongue.

He deepened their kiss, his tongue sweeping deep inside her mouth, taking her as if she were his.

She forgot all about the cut and could only cling to his broad shoulders as he swept her away to where she forgot everything—the cut, her throbbing foot, the violence at the club, the doctor's house she now sat in, the doctor and the other man from Al's gang who were watching.

For a few brief moments she forgot everything else until there was only this kiss and the man who was kissing her.

Suki loved to kiss and had been daydreaming about Frank kissing her for weeks.

Now it was happening.

His kiss took her breath away, and in those moments nothing else existed.

All she could do was kiss him back and let him know how much she wanted him to kiss her.

Her fingers, which had clung to his shoulders,

moved down his arms, feeling the strength of his muscles as they moved, and she would've loved to feel so much more of him.

But the kiss intensified and, all thought aside, she forgot to move her hands.

His hand cupped the back of her neck, reached into her hair and pulled her head slightly back as he pulled away, gazing deep into her eyes with a smoldering heat, letting her know how much he still wanted her and how controlled he was now, breaking the kiss off.

"Save that for me, doll," he said. "To finish later."

Her eyes searched his and she realized the heat between them both, along with the fact he'd be coming back for more of that heat.

Suddenly she came back to herself, back in the room, with both the doctor and the other gangster watching them.

The other man was sitting up now, watching her intently and looking more than interested now that he was bandaged up.

Frank had just marked her as his in front of those two.

Any man who so much as touched her was a dead man.

He just placed protection on me better than him handing me a gun. I might not need to learn how to shoot after all. Word will spread that I'm Frank's girl.

Frank was good with a gun, even those

Thompson submachine guns which were usually erratic and hard to control, because he went to their private range every week to train.

He was quick and accurate and known for it within the gang.

No one was going to mess with his woman.

The doctor peeled off his bloody gloves. "Let me see to that foot now," he said.

He looked at Suki and shook his head at the fancy white dance shoes she had on. "And take those heels off."

She bent down and undid the straps on her dance shoes then slipped them off.

Her right ankle was incredibly swollen and throbbing and happy to have the shoe and ankle strap off.

That did feel better.

The doctor held her foot and examined it without saying anything other than 'does this hurt' each time he tried to move her foot.

"Yes," she answered each time.

Everything did hurt, despite the rum warming her body.

"I'll be back once I make a call." He went into the other room to use the phone just inside on the kitchen wall. He picked up the phone and said, "Ring Sam Weston for me, please."

He waited while the telephone operator made the connection. Then he said, "Hello, Sam?"

He listened for a moment and then said, "Sorry to bother you this late, but I need to borrow your foot-o-scope."

Suki crinkled her forehead and looked at Frank.

What in the world?

"Foot-o-scope?"

Frank shrugged. He obviously didn't know what the doctor wanted to do either.

"I'm sending a man to pick it up. If you can meet him at the store."

He must mean Frank.

"Good. Thanks, Sam."

He hung up and came back into the room to stand in front of Frank. "I need you to go to Weston's Shoes and pick up their foot-o-scope for me. It's that new device they're using to fit shoes."

Suki laughed. "But I don't need new shoes. I just need you to look at my foot."

"If the machine can x-ray your foot to see if a shoe fits then it can x-ray your foot to see if anything is broken."

"Oh, yes." She frowned, and her laugher faded. "Of course."

There's nothing to laugh at. I'm just nervous. And a little tipsy.

"I'll be back, doll," Frank said. "Doc Jones will take good care of you."

Jones couldn't be his real name, could it?

Suki doubted it. Best she didn't know.

She nodded at Frank. "I'll be fine."

"Once the machine is here I'll see to your ankle." The doctor's phone rang, and he turned his attention to Frank again on his way to answer it. "There's ice in the ice box and towels in the drawer next to the sink. Put some ice on her ankle before you go."

He turned away to answer the phone.

Frank nodded and headed toward the kitchen.

When he returned with the ice, he placed it on her ankle. "Better?"

"Yes, thank you," Suki said with an inward hiss as the cold of the ice met with her pain- filled ankle. "Better."

Frank bent and gave her a quick kiss on the lips and then, standing up again, he said, "I am gonna need my jacket back, though."

"Oh. Yeah," Suki said, shrugging out of it.

The room wasn't as cold as the street, and the rum had done wonders to help.

I'm much warmer now.

Frank threw his jacket on, saying, "I'll be back. Sit tight."

Where does he think I'm going to go?

Suki nodded and watched as he headed out the door, got into his car, and drove away.

The large man with the bullet wounds had been watching her.

Without Frank's coat to cover her, she was more exposed in her white dance costume.

His gaze raked her from her head slowly down to her legs. "Nice gams," he said.

Suki nodded. Men always liked her legs. "I'm a dancer."

"Yeah. I saw you. On stage at The Green Mill. You were there tonight."

"Yes, I was."

"You Frank's moll?"

The question came fast, taking Suki by surprise, which likely showed on her face.

He just saw Frank kiss me. It should've been clear.

But maybe Frank kisses all the girls that way. Maybe nothing about me is special to him if he kisses all the girls that way.

We've never even made it to a first date.

It seemed safest to claim Frank's protection, so she nodded. "You think he'd drive just any girl all the way out here?"

The man nodded. "You're one of McGurn's dancers. We take care of our own. But you didn't answer my question."

"Yeah, I'm Frank's girl."

That had yet to be determined, but he'd kissed her and provided her with protection, so Suki was going to make use of that.

He sent her a leering smile. "You get tired of Frank, or you want to switch around at one of them petting parties, let me know."

She wasn't switching at a petting party or

anywhere else. She'd been to petting parties but going to second base with all those eyes watching really wasn't her style.

Even her mother hadn't done that.

Once second base was close, it was time to go back to the apartment.

The swarthy man made her nervous. "Yeah, I'll keep that in mind."

Great. First Mr. McGurn, and now this guy, who didn't even bother to give me his name.

"What's your name?" she had to ask.

Not knowing who she was dealing with, and nameless men like this one, made her nervous.

"Rocco. Now you got to give me yours."

Her thoughts immediately went on the defensive.

I don't "got to" do anything.

She thought the words, but smiled, and forced out her name anyway. "Suki."

"Suki. I like that," Rocco said. "Smooth, like your creamy thighs." He winked.

And your eyes will never see between my thighs.

She kept the words to herself so as not to anger him.

"Try to rest so that wound can heal," the doctor said.

Suki raised Frank's glass and took a good healthy swallow of rum, finishing it off.

Being here with Rocco had made her nervous, but the rum helped.

The doctor checked Rocco's wounds one more time and put a final wrap on them. "You're good to go."

"Thanks, Doc. I think I'll stick around." Rocco's gaze went back to Suki.

"Suit yourself." The doctor went back into the other room, leaving them alone.

She watched his retreating back.

Great. Alone with Rocco. And he's only sticking around because of me. Hurry back, Frank.

CHAPTER 3

*a*fter what seemed like forever, Frank pulled up outside, and Suki let out a breath she hadn't known she held.

She watched through the window as he got out of the car, and picked up and carried in the foot-o-scope, a wooden box four-feet high, and built like a column on someone's fancy porch.

The doctor opened the door and let him in.

He placed the box in front of Suki and the doctor came over to stand beside it.

Frank eyed Rocco. "Still here?"

"Wanted to see what the doc was gonna do with that thing."

"Huh." Frank sounded less than enthused that Rocco was still there, but then he turned his attention to Suki. "How're you holding up, doll?"

"Okay I guess." She shrugged.

She'd had another glass of rum while he was gone and had a slow buzz going. Then she frowned. "I hope it's not broken."

"I hope so, too," he said.

"We'll know soon," the doctor said. "Now, place your foot in the opening."

There were places in the top and sides where the doctor could look in at her foot.

She slid her foot into the box and the doctor looked at her foot from all three directions, moving from one viewing area to the other.

"What can you see?" Curiosity got the best of her and she wished she could see for herself.

She leaned as if to get up to stand on her feet.

"Sit down," Frank and the doctor said at the same time.

"I can see all the bones of your foot and ankle," the doctor said and then stood up again. "And you, little dancer, won't be dancing for a long while. Or standing on it. Your talus bone, that's the big one on the bottom of your foot, is broken in half."

"Oh, no!"

Her thoughts raced.

How will I dance? How will I make rent? It's due in three days. Mrs. Razlo will throw me out. And Tessa, too.

Her roommate, Tessa, didn't have the scratch for Suki to borrow in a pinch, and Mrs. Razlo was the meanest landlady Suki had ever met.

This could put us both out on the street. What will I do?

"Are you listening?" Frank asked as he scowled at her.

The doctor had been talking and she'd missed something.

"I'm sorry, what did you just say?"

"You're lucky it's a clean break. It'll heal well, if you follow directions. You'll be in a cast for six weeks. But that doesn't mean you can walk around on it. I want you to stay off your foot as much as possible."

"Oh no," she groaned. "How am I supposed to do that? My apartment has stairs."

"If you're staying off that foot, you won't be taking those stairs, young lady."

"But how am I supposed to get up there?" Her voice squeaked as her stress level rose. "Or get around? Or even get there?"

"I can take you," Rocco said.

"Don't worry, doll." Frank's warm hand rested possessively on her bare shoulder, giving Rocco a clear signal. "I'll carry you up the stairs, when I take you home," Frank's firm, warm voice combated the stress building inside her.

Suki took a deep breath, and then heaved a deep sigh. Then, closing her eyes, she gave a nod.

Well, the landlady can hardly kick me out if I can't make it down the stairs. Once in, I'll be stuck there. Then what could she do to get me out? But that still doesn't solve the problem of needing to pay her.

Her shoulders sagged. What energy she had left, drained from her, and there was only the constant thudding ache of pain from her ankle despite the rum she'd drunk.

Maybe she needed another swallow.

My ankle is broken. There's nothing I can do. Not one thing.

"Baby, I'll see that you have everything you need," Frank said. "Relax."

Rocco stood to leave now that Frank was clearly prepared to take care of her as his own. "Thanks, Doc."

Rocco tipped his hat, nodded to all three of them, and then was out the door into the dark night.

Suki had no idea where or how, as she hadn't seen another car when they'd parked, nor did she hear one start up, but it didn't matter.

These guys were secretive, and the less you knew about them the better.

Frank was here now, to take care of her, but she had mixed feelings. Even though Frank was being kind and she needed his help, being dependent on anyone didn't sit well with Suki.

She'd been on her own since the day she'd moved out of her mother's place and taken any job she could get just to be able to eat and put a roof over her head.

Not once had she leaned on anyone else to pay her bills.

But at least Rocco was gone now. Likely he'd leave her alone when he saw her again.

Word would spread that she was under Frank's protection and no one would bother her after tonight.

That would be nice.

No more invites from men like Mr. McGurn. Invites that a girl didn't dare turn down.

The doctor turned to go in the other room. "I'll gather everything needed to make your cast."

"How long will I be in a cast?"

"Six weeks."

"That's a long time."

"You want it to heal properly." The doctor left the room to get the materials.

"I'm a dancer. It's how I make my living," Suki said, worry wrinkling her brow.

"You need to follow doctor's orders," Frank said.

"I know. But six weeks? It's just too long. This isn't good." She shook her head.

"Try not to worry about that right now, doll. Take it one step at a time."

"One step." Suki laughed. "You're funny, Frank."

"Yeah. I'm a real funny guy."

She watched him, wondering if he had a great sense of humor, or if he was being sarcastic, or both.

What would his humorous side be like?

She'd only seen his serious protective side until now, and there wasn't much room for humor in his job working for Mr. Capone.

But what was he like when he was down to his t-shirt and boxer shorts?

That image clicked into her mind and she knew she'd return to it often, remembering the way he'd kissed her.

The doctor returned with the makings of her cast. "All right, now. Ready?"

She took another sip of the new drink Frank had just poured her and nodded.

Frank pulled up a chair to sit beside her and took his hand in hers.

It was comforting having him hold her hand and it was a comfort she wasn't used to.

No one had ever just sat and held her hand before.

The doctor proceeded to remove her torn stocking, rolling it down her leg as if it were something he did every day.

And who knew? He might've. He was so matter of fact and unmoved by it. But she guessed he'd seen more on women than their legs. He was all business.

He put her cast together while they sipped on their drinks and watched.

By the time the doctor had finished, she'd sipped her way through several glasses of rum and it had gone to her head, making her dizzy while giving her the giggles.

She was certainly feeling no pain now, only a dull throb and the heavy cast.

"Thanks, Doc," Frank said, and shook his hand. "I'll make sure she follows directions. Will you take the cast off when it's time?"

"Sure. Call first, in case I've been called away."

"You got it." He turned to Suki. "Your chariot awaits, sweet Suki."

She giggled and blushed, the heat from the rum making her face warm. "Then take me home, Frank."

He scooped her up in his arms and she wrapped her arms around his neck again. Breathing in his scent and feeling his strong arms around her, combined with the warm glow of the rum, made her feel all melty inside.

As he carried her toward the car, she nestled against him. "Mmm, this is nice. You smell good and you have strong arms."

"You like this, huh?"

"Yes."

"Good. I like it, too."

Placing her in the car, he closed her door, and went around to his side. He got in and started the car.

She laid her head back against the seat.

"Don't fall asleep on me now," he said. "I need to know where you live."

She rattled off the address without thinking.

"Do you live alone?"

"I have a roommate, Tessa."

"Good. You'll have help when I can't be there."

Her lids heavy, the roar of the engine, and his calm voice lulling her to sleep, her eyes closed. "You'll be there?" She spoke softly.

"Yes. I'll be there."

Her eyes flew open, remembering. "Rocco said he'd step in if you get tired of me."

"Rocco," he ground out slowly, "isn't going anywhere near you."

"He sure was interested."

"Any man would be interested. You're the bee's knees, doll. In case nobody ever told ya."

"Aww, Frank, you're swell." She gave him her warmest smile, but then it faded. "And what happens if he does come near me? Keeps bothering me?"

"First, he's a pussy. Second, any guy bothers you I'll take care of them."

Her eyes widened in silence.

He reached over and ran his finger down her cheek, making her eyes drift closed again. "Go to sleep now," he said. "I'll take you home and wake you when we're there."

She drifted then into a rum-flavored dream as

she relaxed, forgetting all about Rocco, Mr. McGurn, or anyone else.

Frank would take care of her.

Frank would take care of everything.

When Frank pulled up to her address ,and eyed the steps that led from the side of the house up to the second floor, he cursed.

She woke immediately, sitting up. "Oh no," she said, looking frantically around for the gunmen she'd begun to see again, this time in her rum-fueled dream.

His warm hand settled on her leg. "It's all right, doll. Just a lot of steps to go up."

"I can't. Go up them," she said, the rum and the sleep slowing her thought process.

"I know. I told you I'd carry you." He put the 1911 back in his shoulder holster, got out, went around to her side of the car, and opened the door.

"Put your arms around my neck and I'll do the rest."

"Oh, Frank," she said, reaching for him. "You can carry me any time." Her hands went around his neck, and he reached for her, pulling her up, until their faces were so close together their breath inter-mingled.

Breathing in deep, his masculine scent enfolded her as she closed her eyes and tried to make the violent images and sounds in her mind disappear.

Tommy guns and screaming echoed in her mind, from the club and from her dream.

"Hey, sweetheart. Don't go to sleep yet."

"I'm not asleep. I was remembering." She opened her eyes. "Remembering bad things."

He'd noted the way her lashes rested, and the fragility of her face in repose. Her defenses down, she wasn't as spunky as she showed herself to the world at the club. He'd watched her for a while.

She did what she did to keep herself safe. That's what a smart dame did. This one was vulnerable beneath that. It brought out his protective side, and made him want to protect her all the more.

"Bad things."

She was remembering the club and it upset her.

With a driving need to take her mind off the events at the club, along with a deep desire to kiss her, his lips crushed down on her red, kissable lips.

She gasped before kissing him back with fervor.

Damn, she tastes good.

She wasn't all show and tease. This woman could kiss.

Their tongues met and danced.

Coming up for air, he said, "I'm going to put you over my shoulder, so don't wiggle."

"Well, you get a wiggle on then," she said.

"You got it." He grinned. He liked her saucy and full of rum.

She gave a small giggle.

Then up and over his shoulder she went, her sexy ass in the air. He moved to the steps, carrying her, and then they went up, her giggling more than wiggling.

She's cute as a button when she's snockered.

At the top he stopped on the landing and set her down. "Need your key now, babe."

"Oh. It isn't in my bag. We cheese it." She giggled. "Only we mice know where it is."

"Tell me."

She giggled again, the rum making her silly. "Look under the mat."

He gave her a look. "You're kidding, right?"

She shook her head, suddenly going serious. "No."

"That ain't smart, doll."

"There's nothing here to steal," she whispered, making him lean closer to her to hear. "Nothing of value."

He took her chin in his hand, his eyes blazing, and then he kissed her fast and fierce. Breaking the kiss, he said, "There's you."

Her eyes widened as, even in her drunken state his words, hit home. "Oh," she breathed in.

"No more keys under the mat."

"But then Tessa can't get in."

"She can use her own key."

"No, she can't, she lost hers."

"Well she ain't using yours." With that, he bent

down, found the key and opened the door, then pocketed the key.

He went to pick her up again, his low voice rumbling through his chest as he lifted her. "Hold on."

The order and the tone of his voice sent an electric thrill through her.

Oh, he's taking command. That's nice.

The command was one she was happy to comply with as she clung to him for safety and security. Those words, she took to heart. *Hold on.*

She'd never had a man to hold on to before. None had offered, and none would've been safe enough if they had.

His words made her want to hold on to him in more ways than one, and the way he took command and her need to do as he'd said made her trust him enough to obey.

He was taking command of everything and she liked it, very much.

This was new. And fun.

The rum was making it oh, so easy. So easy to just go along with everything and let him take care of her.

Swooping her up, he carried her inside.

In the cold, dark apartment he took in the first room and said, "Where's your room?"

"Second door on the right."

He carried her to it and, pushing open the door

with his foot, he eyed the dark room, which consisted of a bed with a deep red covering, a bedside table and a dressing table. A red-velvet-covered chair was near one window covered with red lace curtains.

He sat her on the bed and moved to turn on the light on the ceiling.

Once the light was on, the room appeared warm, sultry, and welcoming.

She sat watching him. "Frank." She reached out to him and he came near.

"Yes, doll?"

"I want you."

"I know."

He knows.

She watched him, wondering, *How much does he know?*

"I want you right now, but you're too far." She reached a hand out to him and gave him a pout. "You'll have to come to me. I can't walk around in this cast and this shoe." She let her arm drop as she looked down, frowning. "These dogs are done. I can't dance." Her voice broke.

"I know, baby. Try not to think about it."

"Oh, Frank," she said, looking back at him with a furrowed brow. "I don't like this cast." She shook her head. "It's awful. How can I..."

Her voice trailed off as she looked down at it again. "And I want to..."

She looked back up at him. "How can we..."

He was in front of her in a moment, salvaging the mood, taking her hand in his before the drink took her too far in the wrong direction.

"You let me take care of that." He rubbed his thumb across the back of her hand.

She smiled at the caress. "Yes, okay, Frank. You're a swell guy. You've been great. Saved my life, took me to Doc, brought me home..."

He sat as she spoke and then his arm wrapped around her waist as his other hand cupped the back of her neck, moving up her bare neck, up beneath her bobbed hair.

His fingers reached in and gathered her hair, pulling her head back gently but with just enough strength to let her know he meant business.

She lost whatever she'd been about to say next and opened one hand over his chest, tucked her fingers under the lapel of his jacket, and hung on as her other hand rose up to hold the back of his neck. Then she held on for his kiss, wondering if it would sweep her away as it had the last time.

His lips, so near, covered hers, and at the first touch she closed her eyes, only to feel everything. Every insistent and subtle move his lips made, as he made her his.

He tasted so good.

He made her feel tingly all over, the way he touched her, the passion of his kiss, his scent and even the sound of his voice did things to her. Made her feel languid and liquid wanting him.

No man had ever made her go weak in the knees the way Frank did.

It was a heady feeling, this chemistry they had between them and, combined with the alcohol, was quite a mix.

At first intense as he kissed her, he then played lightly with her tongue, brushing his lips over hers once one way and then the other before bringing his tongue back to play, tracing the outside of her lip and then plunging inside again. Teasing her as no man had ever teased her before. Coaxing her to play, until play she did.

She became wanton with her kisses, with her need, her hands clutching at him as her body craved much more than a kiss.

Rum kisses. Oh, how I like them. Want more of them. Want more of him.

She pulled away and stood, holding onto his shoulder with one hand.

Then she reached for the bottom of her white dress where the fringe was attached. Pulling it up and over her head, she popped out from beneath it, watching his eyes and seeing them darken at the sight of her bare breasts.

"Beautiful," he said.

Her smile lifted one corner as she sat on the bed again. L

eaning back on her elbows she said, "Want to see them shimmy?"

"Doll face, I have seen them." He gave her a slow, sexy smile. "Every night for two weeks I've watched you shimmy."

He reached for her breasts.

She leaned her head back, arching for him with a throaty laugh. "Oh, yes, do that. Do everything."

The sight of her leaning back on her elbows, giving herself up for his exploration and enjoyment with the utter abandon of a flapper, made him grin.

He stood to shuck out of his suit, watching her eyes as he unbuckled his belt and drew it slowly out from his pants.

Watching her eyes, he briefly retreated into his thoughts.

This one likes to play, likes to have a good time. Maybe I've finally found a dame who can keep up with me. This one will give as good as she gets. And with her foot as it is, she won't be hitting any dance floors any time soon or going out on the town. Looks like I'll have to bring the party to her.

Best first date I've ever had.

He couldn't keep the grin off his face as he sat to remove his shoes. "So, Suki," he said. "How do you like it? Slow or fast?"

"Depends on my mood," she said. "But I think you might be good at reading my mood." She laughed again. "You can kiss me like you just did any time. Night or day." She laughed low. "Any time. Anywhere."

"That's good." His tone held approval as he stood up and walked over to her.

"Because," he grasped her chin, "I mean to make you mine."

When she didn't answer but just watched him, her expression unreadable, he kissed her again, and she gave herself to him within the kiss, with enthusiasm.

He was more excited than he'd been in a long time.

Suki had him excited more than just sexually. He was feeling protective and dominant. She needed him, and he wanted and needed her. Suki was special.

He'd picked her out of a good-looking selection of dancers. There was just something about her and now he'd make her his, in every way. It made him want to roar like a lion, so the world would know she was his.

He pulled away then and said, "That's a start."

"I like your kisses," she said.

She wasn't committing yet.

Flappers often wouldn't commit. Some never intended to pair up with a man and marry. But this one had been through a few boyfriends from what he had heard.

A man would have to be crazy to give her up.

Now she was under his protection and he would make her his. She was as good as his girl whether she realized it yet or not. They'd talk about that later.

He unbuttoned his shirt and shucked out of it.

She watched him, and her gaze traveled to his arms.

Arms that had been lifting since he was thirteen, until he was no longer that tall, skinny kid. Arms he kept strong by continuing to lift.

She watched him remove his pants until he stood only in his undershirt and boxers.

He pulled the undershirt off and enjoyed seeing the admiration in her eyes as she ran her gaze up and down his torso, noting how he wanted her.

Her smile became playful. "Help me with my stockings?" She smiled a slow, catlike smile. "They'll need to be rolled down slow, you know. French silk is expensive, so we wouldn't want to tear them."

"Doll face, there's only one stocking," he said. "Doc removed the other. Or did you forget? And this one's already torn. Do you want me to help you to remove it?"

"Yes, please."

He moved over to her and climbed onto the bed, reaching for her leg.

Taking hold of it, he thought of his rough hands and how they could tear the stockings she seemed so proud of.

Why was she worried about a pair of silk stockings? I could buy her a hundred pairs.

He propped her up on the bed and started slowly running his hands up her thighs.

I love a woman in stockings.

Suki had the perfect body. She trembled under his touch.

Holding her leg, he kissed it and then ran his hand up and down it, feeling the smooth silk.

Damn, that's sexy. Would feel good wrapped around a man's back. "I like the feel of this. When we make nookie, you can leave your stockings on."

She gasped, "No."

Why is she overreacting? She isn't making sense.

He noted the alarm in her face and then realized maybe she couldn't afford a new pair to replace them.

She'd already ruined the pair she'd worn tonight, though right now, she seemed clueless of that fact. Even though he'd reminded her.

She'd drunk a lot of rum tonight and this concern over stockings was stuck in her head.

Obviously, she needed fancy stockings to do her work as a dancer and they were important to her.

"Do you have any idea what kind of money I make?"

"No." She shook her head.

"Don't worry, doll. Anything you wear that we rip

or tear I'm more than able to replace. Twenty times or one hundred times over."

"Twenty times," she whispered, her blue eyes widening. "No one could afford one hundred times." She gave a little shake of her head, not comprehending what he was trying to tell her.

"Hell, I could afford to take you to Paris to pick them out." He picked up her leg again and kissed it, "Doll face, I'll buy you stockings in every color and style, and enjoy tearing them off you."

Then he teased her by taking the stocking in his teeth. With a growl he gave her a love bite, and then released her. "Right now, I want you to leave this one on."

He reached for a pillow and propped it under the cast on her other foot. "How's that? Comfortable?"

"Yes, but I don't know how we're going to do anything with this stupid thing." She frowned at the cast.

He covered her mouth with his, kissing her hard to make her forget about the cast and her stockings as his hands roamed over her body. Up over her legs and hips, then down to the inside of her thighs, across her ribs and up to her breasts.

His touch left her feeling all kinds of tingly. The passion of his kiss and the way his hands roamed as if they knew just when and where and how to touch made her body ignite.

No man had ever made her weak in the knees

the way Frank did. The touch of his hands created a sensation that made her body come alive.

Watching him through nearly closed eyes, she let herself go.

Who cares about my broken foot? I need Frank now.

Suki forgot everything but Frank and the way he was making her feel. All the while he kissed her, his hands roamed until she nearly couldn't stand any more.

His hand rubbed up her leg.

"I love your thick thighs." His hand ran down her legs again. "Sexy dancer's legs."

"Mm. You're sexy, too." She nearly purred with all the stroking and kissing.

"Bet those legs could wrap around me and never let go."

"Oh, yeah, they could."

Frank began giving her little kisses all down her stomach.

Her muscles gave little twitches.

Slowly Frank took control and she let him, losing herself into the sensations.

He was relentless in his pursuit of their pleasure.

They were both fully sated when he stopped.

"Better?" he asked.

She nodded with a sleepy smile.

"Good."

She felt warm and cuddly, now all that tension had

been released, and suddenly she was sleepy again. Much sleepier than she'd been before. She wanted nothing more than to curl up in his arms right now.

He leaned over and gave her a kiss on the lips. "Good?"

She looked at him through sleepy eyes. "Oh. Frank. Better than good. It was wonderful."

He smiled. "Glad you liked it."

"I loved it."

She smiled a sleepy smile and her lashes drifted closed. "It's real nice, Frank. Real nice."

He pulled the covers up over her, so she could drift off to sleep. Then he pulled on his pants.

"You leaving?" Her eyes had opened again and were now looking at him sleepily.

"No." He sat next to her on the bed. "I'm not going to leave you alone tonight."'

"I'm glad," she murmured, already dozing off to sleep.

"I take care of what's mine, Suki," he said. "You're safe. Go to sleep now."

Satisfied and half asleep already, she didn't answer.

Propped up on the wall, Frank dozed off with his arms wrapped around Suki.

They slept, but it wasn't long before they woke again. Their bodies wanted to connect.

Soon the morning sun was rising.

She'd lost count of how many times they'd made love.

His hand reached over and grasped the covers, pulling them up over her and then pulling her close to wrap his arms around her. "You're cold."

"A little."

He frowned and looked around the small room. "Why do you keep it so cold in here?"

"We have the rent to pay and food to buy and so, heat," she shrugged, "comes lower on the list of things to pay 'cause the other two have to be paid first. The landlady hasn't had the boiler in the basement fixed. She says that will be extra and we don't have it this month."

"That changes now." He got up out of bed and, reaching for his pants, pulled his money clip out of his pocket and then peeled off three C-notes.

Laying them on the dresser, he turned to go into the other room. "Now get it fixed, and turn up the goddamn heat."

Suki lay in bed, clutching the covers and looking at the money on the dresser. So many emotions were rolling inside of her, and the rum buzz was wearing off.

Her emotions were all over the place, with the fresh memories of their time together. The way Frank had made slow love to her at first had made her excited and happy, hungry and needy. Needy for him again and again, until her body had reached a point of exhaustion. What was between them had been pure sex. Pure desire and satisfying that desire.

Emotionally, she suddenly wanted more. Being with him felt right.

The money on the dresser brought in shame, guilt and embarrassment, and mixed it all together. Shame that she wouldn't be able to pay her own bills without his help.

They'd slept together and now he was leaving money right after sex. It made her feel like a street-walker, not a dancer. Like he'd paid her for sex.

She didn't know how to deal with the shame, so she stayed silent. Guilt that she'd abandoned her vow to never to be like her mother had surfaced. For what did all those "uncles" do but the very same thing Frank had just done?

I'll never be like my mother, she vowed again, but it felt hollow this time. She watched for Frank to come back into the room.

Embarrassment spread through her.

He didn't seem as affected by their lovemaking as she.

It had felt like the start of a relationship until he'd left the C- notes.

Regret crept in. She couldn't do this again, though she very much wanted to spend another night in his arms. She'd like that very much once her body was rested again.

He's ruined it by leaving money.

Money she couldn't afford to turn down. If she did, she'd be on the nut. And it was cold outside.

I can't let this happen again. I'm not going to be a kept woman. I'll heal my foot and then be back dancing and earning my own keep. This is a temporary, one-time thing.

But now we've been this close, what will it be like between us?

Nookie with a man changes everything. Even if you don't want it to.

It's not like I'll ever forget this night. This was the best sex of my life and Frank saved my life. It's been wonderful, and now he's ruined it with money.

Silent, she still didn't know what to say or do. She heard him in the kitchen, looking around.

He must be hungry.

She was.

Was there even any food in the apartment?

When the girls had men over, food usually wasn't involved.

Suki's mother had always said, "If you want to make sure a man comes back, be sure to feed him real good. If you feed them, they'll return."

Suki hadn't met a man yet that she wanted returning again and again. And she knew from watching her mother, that the last thing she'd ever want was a man who wouldn't go, when she told him to go.

Do not feed the boyfriends. It was a policy Suki and Tessa agreed on.

"Heck, they should buy us dinner," Tessa said. "We're working women. If he wants a domestic sort of girl, he shouldn't pick a flapper."

Suki had no interest in cooking. For anyone. Nor did she want to get married. There was too much of life to see and do and she wanted to see and do it all, not be shackled to some man and told what to do or not to do.

Curling onto her side, she noted her skin felt overly warm and more sensitive than usual, especially in certain places.

She blushed at the memory of some of the things they'd done. Things she'd never heard of.

And she'd thought there was nothing new. But Frank was creative in bed.

The unusual electricity between them heightened everything and she simply felt more. More alive and more sated then she'd known she could be.

If she could just get a handle on her emotions. She lay there thinking until she came to a decision.

Life is short and I'm going to live it. I want to feel alive. I want to feel everything. Every single thing. And to try everything, too. And so, I will.

And right now, I want Frank. In my bed, doing those things again. He'll want that, too. I won't think about the rest right now.

I need my foot to heal and then I'll decide what next.

For now, I'm just going to live a little. Accept new stockings. Turn up the heat. And tell Frank he can come over again and do that thing he does with his tongue so well.

I'll just live in the now. In the right now. And not worry about tomorrow.

He came into the room with two bologna sandwiches on white bread and a pitcher of water. Placing them on the bedside table, he said, "One slice of bologna on two pieces of thin bread. Doll, you've got to eat better than that." He shook his head. "I'll bring food next time I come, and I'll cook."

"You cook?" The thought hadn't even occurred to her.

Frank, the big, tough enforcer could cook? Wanted to cook dinner?

This was a first.

"I'm Italian." He laughed. "What do you think?" He shook his head. "Of course, I cook."

Oh, lord. She watched him with wide eyes. *I must've died and gone to heaven.*

"So, you could make spaghetti," she said.

"I can make a whole lot more than spaghetti."

"I love spaghetti."

"Then you will have it."

He leaned forward, placing a soft kiss upon her lips, surprising her with the gentle touch.

She sighed into it. "You're spoiling me."

"I intend to." He handed her a sandwich. "Eat."

She took a bite and then they both ate in silence, having built up appetites.

"Now it's late. I got to go."

"Okay." She yawned.

He placed a piece of paper on the bedside table. "This is my number. Call if you need me. And no walking on that foot."

He waited for her to answer.

"Okay, Frank."

All she wanted was sleep. She was too tired for anything else. He'd exhausted her.

This bossy tendency of his, she'd let it go for now.

They could work out who was in charge of what later.

I'm not really under his thumb; I'm just living in the right now.

CHAPTER 4

*T*he next day Frank was back, after Tessa left for work at the diner.

She'd pulled a double shift yesterday and so had missed Suki and seeing her injury until this morning when Suki hobbled out, making her way to the bathroom with bleary eyes and a hovering hangover.

Suki held up a hand, not wanting to speak until she'd made the morning bathroom dash, which was as far from a dash as she'd ever been, on her crutches.

She'd never been much of a morning person, unlike Tessa. But then Tessa often had to work the breakfast shift if she was working a double and Suki always worked at night.

Mostly they saw each other coming and going and they both liked it that way. Especially if one of them had a boyfriend over. Which they really weren't supposed to do, but the landlady didn't have it written into the lease so, as Suki said, the woman could hardly enforce it.

The moment she'd come out of the bathroom, Tessa was waiting. "What happened to you?" Concern filled her face.

"There was shooting at the club last night. I was running down the stairs when I fell and broke my ankle. But Frank took me to the doctor after he saved my life. The doctor fixed me up and then Frank brought me home."

Tessa gave Suki the once over and said, "Did more than brought you home, it looks like. Well, I'm glad you're okay and didn't get shot. What are you gonna do now?"

"I have to stay off my foot for six weeks."

Tessa frowned. "There's no way you can dance."

"I know." Suki started to hobble to her room. "I didn't expect to be on the nut. But," she shrugged, "there it is.

"You're broke." Tessa frowned. "What are you gonna do now?"

"Frank gave me some money. We can pay rent and there's extra to fix the boiler in the basement, so we can have decent heat for a change. He wants the heat turned up and kept up."

"Well, hell, that's fine with me as long as he's paying for it. I get tired of piling on extra clothes and blankets just 'cause we're short every month. If you've found a sugar daddy, try to keep him through the winter."

"I'll keep him until I decide it's time for him to go."

Suki went into her room, grabbed the money off the dresser, and then handed one of the C-notes to Tessa. "Here. For the rent and the boiler repairs and groceries. Since it doesn't look like I'm getting out to run errands any time soon."

Tessa looked down at the money in her hand, her eyes narrowing. She glanced sharply at Suki. "That's a lot of dough. What does Frank do?"

"He works for Al."

"Capone?" Tessa's eyebrows shot up.

"Yeah. The big cheese himself."

"Be careful." Concern slid over Tessa's face.

"I will."

"It might not be so easy to tell him to go, if you decide it's time."

"I'll be fine." Suki held a hand up, signaling she was done talking.

Tessa placed the money in her pocket. "Thanks, Suki. I'll pay the rent on my way out and take care of the heat bill, too. We'll have these rooms toasty in here before long. Now, shouldn't you be back in bed off your foot?"

"Yeah, I'm just gonna sleep. I'm tired." She moved toward her room and then looked over her shoulder. "Oh, hey, use some of that to have a new key made for yourself. Frank doesn't want us leaving one under the mat anymore."

"Okay by me. Frank got a last name?"

"It's Omato."

"Haven't heard of him. Well, I'm sure I'll get to meet him if he's going to be calling on you. Just let me know if you want me to be scarce or if you want me to check on you."

"I'll be fine. Thanks, Tessa."

"All right. I'm off to work, then. Get some rest. You look like hell."

"I didn't get much sleep last night." Suki went into her room and sat on the bed and positioned her cast before leaning back. "Don't wake me if you're home early," she called out.

"I won't," Tessa called back. "Call me at the restaurant if you need anything."

"I will," Suki answered and then closed her eyes as she relaxed into her pillow. Hearing Tessa leave and close the door barely registered as Suki's thoughts were back on Frank.

Tall, dark, and handsome Frank, who'd saved her from death last night and had seen that her foot was taken care of and then taken her home.

The kisses and the sex had been incredible. Maybe she'd dream of Frank kissing her again, making her forget the heavy clunky cast and the foot that was now throbbing again.

I need more of that rum. Too bad I don't have any.

With that thought, she dozed.

Frank's heavy footsteps echoed down the hall, waking her before she heard his voice. "Suki, you awake?"

"Mm-hmm." She rubbed sleep from her eyes before sitting up.

"I brought food."

"Mm, good. I'm hungry."

"You ought to be, if all you've had was a bologna sandwich. That was a long time ago."

Her stomach growled in answer.

"I'll just put the food away." He went into the kitchen and she listened to the sounds of the fridge and the cabinets opening and closing again.

When he returned he held a plate of olives and cheese and carried a brown bag. He placed the plate on the bed and then sat on the other side of it.

Her stomach growled.

"Eat," he said.

She reached for a slice of cheese and asked the questions that had been on her mind.

Questions she should've asked last night.

"Who were those men, Frank? Why did they want to kill Mr. Capone? Why would they come into the club like that?"

"You ask a lot of questions. Eat."

She took a bite of her cheese and he watched her for a moment.

"I just want to know what's going on," she said

after she finished the cheese. "I could've been killed last night."

"But you weren't."

"If you hadn't pushed me out of the way..." She gazed at him with admiration in her eyes. "You saved my life, Frank. Thank you."

He nodded. "No problem, doll."

He spoke as if it was no big thing and was something he did every day.

Taking an olive, he held it out to her and she opened her mouth and took it.

Everything tasted so good.

"I'd still like to know who came into the club shooting." She reached for another olive, popping it into her mouth.

"Probably Northsiders," he said. "On January 12th, the Northsiders shot up Mr. Capone's car."

"I heard about that. At the Hawthorne restaurant, wasn't it?"

"Yeah, that's the place. They shot into the restaurant. Tore the place up. Thompson sub-machine guns can do a lot of damage, but they're not real accurate and they pull up. Luckily, no one was killed."

"How bad was it?"

"Boss's Cadillac looks like a colander. Riddled with holes."

"Not the pretty cream-colored one?"

He nodded. "That's the one."

"It's such a pretty car."

"Not anymore."

"That's a shame."

"He can buy another one. Now, eat."

She took another piece of cheese. "So, you think these were the same guys?"

"No. Different guys. No one recognized them. That's one reason they walked into the club so easily. The other is, one of their gang bought our guy on the door. Or they'd never have got that far. He should've stopped them first."

Frank pointed to the plate. She took a third piece of cheese. "So, who do you think did it?"

"Torpedoes."

"Torpedoes?"

"Ya know, hired guns. From Sicily. That's why we'd never seen them before."

"Why would they come here and shoot up the club?"

"Someone took out a hit on Al and paid off the guy on the door."

"Oh, I hadn't thought of that."

"Doll face, you're a little bit slow." He then ran a slow hand up her thigh.

"How do you think they got in? Should never have gotten past him." He kept moving his hand up, so he could touch more of her as he talked.

"I just woke up when you got here," she said. "That's why I'm slow. I've been sleeping."

Her voice changed as his hands moved across her body and he slid her nightgown up above her waist.

"Some things are good slow. Nice and slow." She looked at him beneath lowered lids, her eyes softening as desire built in her body, as his fingers continued to move. Touching. Teasing.

"I like looking at you. On the stage. On this bed. Ready and waiting for me." His warm hand continued to move across her body, bringing every inch of skin alive as he touched her. "I like knowing you're here, in this bed, waiting. And I like touching you. Slow." He smiled.

"I like that, too."

Taking an olive, he placed it on her belly button. "See how you like this." He then began kissing his way toward it before lapping it into his mouth with his tongue.

Soon the plate and the rest of the cheese and olives were on the floor, along with their clothes, while he kissed nearly every inch of her body.

No flame of desire had ever lit as quickly between her and any other man as it did with Frank. Yet he kept moving slow.

She lost track of time as he built the need in her.

Frank knew his way around a woman's body and took her to places she'd never been before. He was that good and she wasn't exactly new at nookie.

Finally, both were exhausted.

She lay panting, and he rolled over to lie beside her after reaching in his coat pocket for a cigarette.

The pack said Lucky Strike, which was a brand she also liked.

"Cig?"

"Sure," she said. Her pack was in her coat pocket back at the club.

"I thought you might be out," he said.

"Mine are still at the club."

He handed her the cigarette and then struck a match and lit it for her. They smoked in companionable silence. Then he got up and went into the other room.

Even the best round of sex had an ending and now she was sticky, salty, and spent.

She lay on her back, staring at her dressing table mirror, and feeling less than pretty. She didn't usually let men hang around long enough to see how she looked in less than glamorous situations, and she hadn't even had a bath since she'd dressed for the club yesterday. God only knew what her makeup looked like.

It was never good to let a man in too close.

They'd soon take you for granted if you didn't fix up and put your best face on. Then some shiny, pretty little thing would turn their head because she had put hers on, and you weren't so shiny any more.

Men were too often like raccoons. Off for the next

shiny thing. Forgetting the one they'd just held in their hands and thought was their most precious treasure.

When he came back into the room, she decided to ask for help. Much as it irked her to have the need for help, the cast was a reality until it was removed.

"I really need a bath. But I don't know how to take one with this thing." She gestured to her cast, which was already starting to get on her nerves before she'd even had it on two full days. It was far from shiny. Nothing about her felt shiny right now.

"I'll help you. And then you can wear the new pajamas I brought you."

"You brought me pajamas?"

"Yeah. Stay here." He winked.

"I'm not likely to be going anywhere soon. But I can't stay here in this bed forever."

He went into the other room without commenting.

When he returned with a package she sat up, excited about the gift.

This is different than him leaving money. This is something he picked out, something thoughtful. Just for me. That made it personal.

He handed her the package.

She hurried to open it.

Inside was a pair of black silk pajamas with red roses on the front.

"Oh, they're stunning," she said.

"Goes with your hair and your lips."

So, it does, she thought. *Soon I'll be shiny again, wearing his gift.*

"Oh, I love them, Frank," she laughed. "Thank you!"

"Come on, I'll help you take a bath and then we'll eat something light before the main meal to tide you over while I finish cooking."

"Oh, Frank, that sounds wonderful." As he helped her up she put her arms around him and said, "You really are spoiling me."

"Doll face, you ain't seen nothing yet. I also brought you some rum."

"Oh, that's swell, Frank. My new favorite drink and I didn't have any. But now I have my own bottle."

THE DAYS SOON RAN TOGETHER, as he came by every single day. Sometimes in the morning and sometimes at night. Days full of gifts, of silk bedclothes and roses and jewelry, of meals and kisses shared, and wild sex across the bed, in the bathroom, on the kitchen table and on the living room couch. Through it all ran the taste of spiced rum, her new favorite drink, which he kept her supplied with, in the silver flask he'd given her with her initials on it.

The sounds of jazz playing spread through the apartment as he brought her new records with all the latest jazz songs.

She lounged in silk pajamas or a silk robe and nothing beneath and she was always waiting for him. It felt decadent and sensual living in nothing but silk day after day.

She was wearing one of the new silk nightgowns he'd brought her last time, saying as he always said, that there was no point in her getting dressed every day while she was healing.

This gown was pale silver silk. She tilted her head and looked at him beneath lowered lashes, and her voice came out with a throaty, "You like?"

"I like." He smiled. "I'll like it even better when it's on the floor."

She laughed, slid out of the nightgown, and tossed it to a nearby chair, saying, "Or over the back of a chair."

"I like seeing you on your back," he said. "Ready and waiting for me. Or bent over the chair waiting and ready."

"More than ready," she said, leaning back. "Come and get me."

"I'll take everything you've got and more, babe," he growled as he moved toward her. "I'll always take what's mine." He smelled of gunpowder and she knew he'd been shooting. Whether at target practice on the private range or in a real shootout, she didn't know and wouldn't ask.

She never questioned what he did when he was gone longer than usual, or when he came to her at odd hours, pouring them both a glass of rum and waiting for her to drink it down before he nearly tore her clothes off. Then it was hard and fast and all about him, while her place was to be ready and willing.

The rougher side of being a gangster's moll emerged during those times, and he wouldn't be slow or thoughtful of her needs until he'd spent whatever wildness inside of him needed to be spent. Only then would he return to the strong thoughtful man who'd cared for her in their first two days together.

She knew she had it better than some, for he never hit her, and when in a generous mood would shower her with gifts as if she were his princess.

He was a very happy man as long as she did what he wanted.

If he lost his temper, he'd replace anything he'd broken, and if his words sometimes stung, well, that was the drink talking.

She liked a drink, too. It made everything hurt less.

When she had a difficult day or evening, there was always the rum. Spiced rum from Jamaica was her new vice, and if she couldn't dance she'd drink and wear her silks and her pearls, while her bed was her new stage and Frank her new man and audience.

She learned to please him, and he spent his

spare time with her, instead of chasing other women.

If asked, both would have said they were happy.

THE LESSONS in pleasing him began within the first week Suki was homebound.

Tessa had been called out to work her shift and overtime, which she'd said she couldn't turn down if Suki wasn't bringing in any money from the club.

Suki didn't blame Tessa, but it left Suki alone to fend for herself, instead of what Frank and Tessa had discussed. The hours she was supposed to be available, she wasn't. So, Suki was handling things herself.

She didn't feel she needed a babysitter and had told Tessa so.

Tessa agreed.

All had been fine until she'd made one trip to the bathroom too many and needed another glass of water and something to eat. She'd decided to sit in the kitchen and stay there until it was almost time for Frank to arrive. And then she'd hobble back into the living room before he came in. Not bothering to dress, she lumbered about the kitchen in her short, pale pink silk chemise. She'd decided to fix a sandwich and eat it at the kitchen table.

Frank stood in the doorway, a thunderous look

on his face, as he'd seen her hobble from the kitchen to lean on the doorframe before she'd stopped short, frozen in surprise.

He slammed the door shut. "What are you doing up?"

"Oh!" she squeaked. "You startled me."

He wasn't supposed to be here this soon. I thought I'd have more time.

With bold strides, he moved forward until he now towered over her, his gaze down on her intense. "Walking on that foot. Is this what you do when I'm not here? I ought to take you over my knee right now for not listening to the doctor and not taking care of yourself. No crutches and not keeping that foot up, which is *not* what the doctor told you to do. You ought to be spanked."

Instead of frightening her, the thought aroused her. He was so masculine and so much in command right then, he made her weak in the knees.

Over his knee? Spanked?

She swallowed hard, her eyes wide looking up at him.

Thoughts of his strong warm hand connecting with her backside gave her a warm feeling and made her eyes widen.

Her response was not lost on him as his gaze took her in.

She shook her head no, but her wide eyes and her sudden arousal was evident to them both.

"You like that idea." His eyes darkened. "It appears you like it a lot."

Unable to answer him for the first time ever, she swallowed again, blushing.

"You can't even answer me."

Blushing was another first for him to see.

Usually she was uninhibited as sex wasn't new to her and she was just as likely to initiate as to wait for a man to do it.

Reading all the signs she was putting out and as she'd not said no to anything he'd suggested, he then took total charge. "I'm going to take your lack of an answer as a yes. You need to be disciplined for your own good."

He hefted her over his shoulder, and then carried her into the other room, saying, "I won't have you injuring yourself because you won't follow doctor's orders. So, I'm going to make sure you don't forget."

Frank!" she yelled.

"What? Close your mouth, woman," he said, "Or you'll get more than a spanking." He swatted her behind.

Oh, he did not just tell me to shut up. That had better be part of the game.

Well, he's never done that before.

What will he do now?

She quieted, wondering about the spanking as curiosity took over.

She'd never in her life had a spanking. Her mother hadn't allowed it. It was the one rule, which had likely spared Suki from unwanted attention from the uncles who were in and out of her mother's life.

With no father around and a mother who was too busy to pay much attention to Suki, she'd been allowed to do what she wanted as long as she stayed quiet and out of the way.

What would a spanking from Frank be like?

She was so curious she could hardly stand it. She'd missed out on spankings. Now she was going to experience one.

Placing her on the bed, he then sat and pulled her over to him until she was across his lap. Pulling her silky clothing away, he bared her buttocks to the air and then ran a hand across one cheek and then the other. "Such sweet round cheeks. Let's see how rosy they are when I'm done."

His hand had warmed them up and then he pulled his hand away and landed it.

Smack.

She jumped and then froze, anticipating the next one.

It didn't come as he sat watching her reaction, waiting.

As she waited, anticipating, wishing he'd hurry, wanting to squirm, desire built, and with each repeated spank followed by the waiting, desire built until she thought she could bear it no more.

Then he pulled her up and kissed her hard on the mouth.

"Are you going to listen to me next time?"

"Yes."

"I only want what's best for you."

"I know."

It actually felt good to know he cared that much, and she was surprised at how much she'd liked the spanking.

They'd moved into a whole new area for her, one she wouldn't examine right now, as she just wanted him to remove his clothes and get on with it.

"Thank you. Now hurry up and get naked. I really need you right now."

"You really want it, do you?"

"Oh, yes, I do."

"Are you going to behave from now on?"

"Sure, Frank."

She smiled, thinking, *until I want another spanking.*

From the look in his eyes, he might've guessed what she was thinking. But then he was shucking out of his clothes, getting ready to give her what she wanted.

Within minutes they were both naked and making the bed rock with energy she hadn't had all day.

He brought out her wild side. This wasn't something anyone else brought out in her to such a large degree, and it surprised her, but she was going with it and living her life in the moment.

She enjoyed living the life of a flapper and to her it meant living in the moment and trying new things. It didn't mean any kind of permanence anyhow.

Nothing was ever permanent.

Suki didn't do permanence.

Independence meant never having to listen to anyone unless they'd hired her.

But a bit of spanking now and again, that would be good. Spanking livened things up in a way nothing else did. Yes, a bit of spanking now and again, if I'm in the mood for it, that would be all right.

AFTER FOUR WEEKS of being apartment-bound, Suki was going stir crazy. She'd been walking around the apartment talking to herself, as there was no one else to talk to, tossing silken clothing on her dressing table and chair until there was a huge mound piled there.

How many silk things did one woman need?

She knew she was being ungrateful, but right now she didn't care.

Isn't there more to life than dressing in silks and

lounging about waiting for a man to come and liven things up?

I'm going out of my mind here. This apartment has started to feel like a cage.

I want to be outside, in the fresh air. Even if it is cold.

I want to go somewhere, anywhere.

I need to get out of this apartment soon.

She missed dancing, and she missed the club and the nightlife and just getting out and going somewhere.

Her roommate, Tessa, was home less, because she had a new boyfriend and went to his place, which made for lonelier days and evenings for Suki.

She missed girl talk, about men and dancing, and picking out dresses together when they went shopping. She missed going out and she missed talking to people.

Other than Frank and Tessa, she hadn't seen one other person since he'd carried her up the stairs.

It was no good being home all the time, when the only one who came to see her was Frank.

She needed girl time.

It can't be all about him every day.

No one came around except Frank, and he really didn't want other people being around. Making that clear, there was little reason for her roommate to stick around, even if she had the time.

And Suki had never invited other dancers over;

she didn't invite people in, she went out. So, all this staying in, now grated on her.

She was moving about the room with her cast and no crutches when Frank came through the front door, big as life and roaring at her.

"What the hell are you doing, Suki? Do I have to bend you over again, for a harder spanking this time?"

"I can't stand it Frank." Her words came out in a rush. "I can't stand being cooped up in this apartment one day more."

He stood with his hands on his hips, scowling at her without saying a word, as his mood swiftly changed to something she couldn't name.

She watched him, trying to gauge his mood.

Something was clearly on his mind and she couldn't read it, or him. Shades of her childhood rose within her.

It could be dangerous if you couldn't read a man's mood.

Was this good or bad? Dangerous or safe?

CHAPTER 5

$\mathcal{F}$rom the thunderous look on his face, she surely didn't want him spanking her today.

She didn't know if he was safe right now, or not. None of the experiences of her past had taught her how to read him.

It was best to be safe.

She held up a hand toward him. "No, please, no spanking."

"You deserve one," he growled. "You don't do as you're told. Doc wanted you off that foot for six weeks. Not three. Not four. Six."

"I know." She moved, backing into a chair, putting her hands on it and then sitting down. "I'm sitting."

He'd crossed his arms as he watched her but had yet to remove the scowl. "You got a suitcase?"

"Why yes, of course. I have two. Though I've only used them once. Why?"

He moved into the kitchen and poured them both a glass of rum. Carrying two glasses back into the front room, he handed hers to her. He still hadn't answered her.

She took a nervous sip and then when he sipped his and watched her over the rim, she took a bigger swallow.

What is he going to do? And why does he want to know if I have a suitcase? Does he want to send me somewhere or take me somewhere?

"You're going stir crazy in this apartment. Cabin fever. And I'm not having you hurt yourself because you can't follow directions."

He finished his glass and then set it on the table hard and stood. "Pack your bags, doll, we're going to Miami."

Miami? Her mind raced. *He wants to take me to Miami? I've never been out of Chicago.*

"Oh, Frank!" She clapped her hands in delight. "How many days?"

"I'm gonna put you up down there, till your foot is healed," he said. "However long that is. You can lounge by the pool and drink mimosas."

"Sounds divine." Already she was envisioning warm sunshine and Florida breezes, away from the cold winds of Chicago. "Thank you, Frank. When do we leave?"

"I'm going to send you ahead."

"Oh." She pouted. "You're not coming with me?"

"No, doll. I have to come down with Al."

Her pout grew bigger and he leaned close.

"Stick that out some more and I'll bite it."

She laughed and did just that, sticking her lip out more, teasing him.

He captured her lip between his teeth and bit once, hard. It wasn't nearly so funny, now that he'd done it. But then he kissed her hard and she almost forgot about the bite.

"You go get settled in at the hotel and pamper yourself. Get a massage, order room service, get your cast off, buy a new dress, and get your hair done, the works." Frank smiled. "Anything you want, doll. I told ya I'd take care of ya. Put it on my room tab and I'll take care of it. Me and the boys will be down with Al in a week or two."

"Oh, Frank, that's swell." She smiled back. "How will I get there?"

"You'll take the train. Pullman sleeper car and no visitors. And you don't tell nobody Al and the boys are coming, you hear? You stay clammed up tight."

"Of course not, Frank. My lips are sealed tight as a clam."

"That's my girl." He held out a hand. "Now, come here."

She stood and moved toward him, and he sat and pulled her onto his lap. Sliding his hand up beneath her silk chemise, he said, "You wearing anything under this?"

Giggling, she said, "Wouldn't you like to know."

"I will know," he said, and he smiled as he reached what his fingers were headed for. "That's what I like. Nothing between us. Good girl. Now, give me a kiss."

She leaned in to kiss him and their lips met as desire sparked between them.

That was all it took for them to dive with passion into a deeper kiss as their hands pulled at each other's clothing.

He came up for air and then bent to nip her ear with his teeth. "I'm going to send you off too tired to even think of sex until I get there."

"Oh, good," she breathed. "I hope you'll join me there, soon."

His fingers moved across her body while he talked. "Be glad Al wants to take this trip. You won't need a winter coat down there."

"What will I need, Frank? I don't know how to... oh. Oh." Her breathing changed, and she forgot what she was going to say.

"What, baby? 'Oh', what?"

"How to pack." She breathed the words out, fast. "For this."

He stopped and then kissed her lips again, abandoning the tease of her body, so she could pay attention.

"There's a new track in Hialeah. Al wants to get out of this weather and check out the ponies at The Miami Jockey Club at Hialeah Park. So, you'll need clothes to wear to the track. Other than that, you can stay like this. Or wear one of the silk things I got you. If we go out, it will be where Al goes. Maybe a party, maybe dinner out."

"The Miami Jockey Club," she said. "I haven't heard of that one."

"It's new," he said. "Just opened in January."

"Oh, I can't wait to see it."

"They got a one-mile dirt track and twenty one stables. This is gonna be something to see. And you'll like this. They got a dance hall."

"But you know I can't dance right now, Frank."

"Don't interrupt me when I'm telling you what's up."

"Okay, Frank."

He held up a finger and she realized she'd interrupted him again.

"I was starting to say, they got the first Spanish Jai Lai in the U.S., and a roller coaster. They even got a snake catcher."

"Wow. A roller coaster? That sounds fantastic, Frank," she squealed. "I can't wait to see it."

"You'll see it all when I take you there. But, you'll see Florida before I will. Take summer clothes and a bathing suit. You leave tomorrow on the train." He took her tickets out of his pocket and laid them on the table. "I'll make sure you're well taken care of. First class all the way. Nothing but the best for my girl."

"Oh, thank you, Frank." She threw her arms around him.

"How 'bout you thank me in the bedroom," he said. "You know what I like."

"Sure, Frank. I sure do." She leaned forward and kissed him.

He helped her into the bedroom and shucked her out of her chemise, and then she was naked in bed, watching him undress and thinking how good he'd look in a swimsuit by the pool.

She wasn't going to think about how she wouldn't be able to swim in that pool.

He'd said she'd stay till the cast was off, and once it was off she planned to swim.

"How did I ever get so lucky?" she asked. "You saved my life, found a doctor, brought me home, have been taking care of me. And now we're going to Miami. You're spoiling me."

"You ain't seen nothing yet, babe. Stick with me and I'll show ya the world."

"Oh, Frank." Her arms slid around his neck. "You can show me the world right here."

Afterward, she lay curled in his arms, thinking and tracing a few of his chest hairs with her finger. "Frank?"

"Yeah, doll?"

"Why do they need a snake catcher?"

She'd been so excited by what they were doing, she hadn't registered the thought fully that they had a snake catcher, but it had stuck in the back of her mind, waiting like a snake, coiled and ready to spring.

"The club is on the edge of the Everglades. Lots of snakes down there."

"Lots of snakes?" Her voice rose.

"Oh, yeah. They might catch twelve a day there's so many."

"Eww." She shivered as goose bumps spread across her skin at the thought of all those snakes. "I don't like snakes. I mean, they scare me, Frank. More than give me the heebie jeebies. They really scare me."

"Most women don't like snakes."

"I know, but I really, really don't like them. They scare me so."

"You're not going to be anywhere near any snakes. So don't worry about it."

His tongue teased her earlobe and then slipped inside her ear, teasing, making her forget snakes.

Then he whispered in her ear, "Now, pay attention. You have three rules on the train," Frank said. "One. No other men. Two. Stay in your room. Three. Touch yourself and think of me, while you are looking out the window at the scenery passing by.

And when I meet you in Miami I want you to be ready and waiting for me."

"Yes, Frank," she said.

The rules weren't hard.

She didn't want another man.

As to the rest, she'd done nothing since breaking her foot but sleep, bathe, eat, get ready for Frank, and be spoiled by him.

After four weeks of constant lovemaking, her body craved his. She thought of Frank constantly.

In just four weeks her world had become all about Frank.

It was easy to do what he wanted, because he hadn't asked her to do anything she didn't already want to do. This was an agreement she could make. He was, after all, paying for the trip, and his rules would be easy to follow.

She'd stopped thinking about what she'd do after her foot healed, how she'd support herself.

The way Frank showered her with gifts and money and now this trip, everything else slid into the background as she was caught up in living in the here and now.

It had always been her way to live in the here and now.

Yesterday was gone and tomorrow might not get here. But there was always now.

And now they were going to Miami. Life with

Frank was a ball so far, and one she never wanted to stop dancing.

When the cast came off, things would change, but she'd think about that then.

She'd never in her life had a day when she didn't worry about money, until Frank. Slipping into this new lifestyle had eased her mind.

"I'm excited about this trip, Frank," she said. "I've never taken the train or been to Miami. I've never even left Chicago."

"You'll be safe on the train in your compartment." He tapped his finger to her nose. "You know to keep your nose to yourself, and don't talk about Al, or answer any questions about us."

She nodded. That was a given.

"My guy Enzo is gonna meet you at the station in Miami. He'll take you to the hotel. The concierge knows about your foot. Anything you need you just ask them, and they'll get it. You can enjoy the hotel till I get there."

"When will you get there?"

"Not sure yet. I'll let you know once you're there. I'll call ya and check on ya. You just be ready when I tell ya I'm on the way."

"Okay, Frank. Will we have much time together with you having to be with Al?"

"Doll, you know when I'm not workin' I'll find you. We'll have a real good time."

"I know."

"There'll be other dames, you can have girl time. I'll introduce you to the right people. You won't be lonely. Entertain yourself till I get there and behave. Like you do here at home."

"Okay."

"Now, how about we have another drink and then you can thank me again for this trip. Gonna be a while before either of us gets any nookie."

"Okay, Frank. I'm thirsty, too. Oh. Can I bring rum on the train?"

"I'll tuck a bottle of your favorite spiced rum into your suitcase. No problem, doll."

"Thank you, Frank. The rum helps my foot hurt less."

"Tastes pretty good, too, doesn't it?"

"Yes. It does."

"You know, that's where the rum comes from."

"Where?"

"Miami. They bring it up through the Keys and then we get it from Miami. So, you can get hooch down there, if you know where to go. But I'll bring ya enough for the trip."

"Oh, that's exciting. Your work is interesting, Frank."

"Yeah, well, best you don't know much more."

She nodded. "Yes. I'm hungry. Bring me a piece of chicken?"

"Sure, doll." Frank went into the kitchen and came back with a chicken leg and a glass of rum for her. "Couple of weeks, your cast will be off and then you can wait on me."

"Sure, Frank. I'll be happy to take a turn. You've waited on me a lot."

"I like to feed my woman. But when a man is tired, he likes the woman to see to his needs."

"Sure, Frank. I understand."

He was laying out how he wanted things, once her cast was off.

But that was two weeks away still, and she was living in the now. They could figure it all out later.

"I'll be glad when this cast is off, so that's two of us. And, of course, I'll reciprocate after you've been taking such good care of me."

"Good. Now, I got to make a call. You eat, and I'll be back."

After they both ate and talked some more, he said, "You've got a big day tomorrow. I'll be here at eight a.m., so be ready."

"Oh, I'll be ready, Frank. I can't wait to see Miami. And to ride on a train."

"Stick with me, doll. I'll take you places you ain't never seen. I take care of what's mine."

"Am I part of what's yours?"

He put a finger under her chin. "What do you think? Ain't you figured that out by now?"

She smiled. "I think I might be."

"Ain't no might about it. You're mine." His tone brooked no argument and made it final.

"Yes, I suppose I am."

"And don't forget it." He let loose of her chin. "You got all the way to Miami to think about it. You'll be traveling first class and you'll have a private room where you'll sleep."

He held up his index finger to emphasize his next words and pointed it at her. "Stay in your room. The porter will bring whatever you need. There's no reason to leave your room."

"But I'm on the train for three days, and I'll need to go to the dining car to eat."

"The porter will bring your meals, and even cook to order for you."

He shook his finger at her. "You'll not entertain other men. You're mine and mine alone."

"Of course, Frank. What kind of woman do you think I am?"

"Just don't need no misunderstandings. I'm telling you now, so there won't be."

"Frank, I've always been a one man at a time kind of woman. I don't need another man."

"In Miami, men will try to woo you. I don't want nothing bad to happen to you."

"Nothing bad is gonna happen, Frank. I've been taking care of myself for a long time."

"Now you don't have to. My guy will take you anywhere you need to go."

"Right. Enzo."

You mean my warden.

She kept the thought to herself.

Once again, he thought she needed a babysitter. It was frustrating, but she didn't want their last time together tonight to be a fight.

Once in Miami, I'll do what I want. It's time to bring the old Suki back, and Miami is just the place to do it.

"Find a doc down there to take that cast off when it's time. But stay off that foot."

"Okay, Frank."

"Good. We have an understanding. This is good." He nodded. "Now I got to go. Give me a kiss and then get some sleep."

She leaned toward him with a pucker.

He kissed her long and deep, then he stood, dressed, and headed for the other room for his coat and hat.

Poking his head into her room again, he saw her pulling things out of drawers, to pack. "Thought I told you to sleep."

"I can sleep after I pack."

"No. You'll pack in the morning."

She wasn't going to argue with him, so she crawled back into bed and pulled the covers up.

I'll wait till he's gone and then pack I'll everything I have. Because, what if I like Miami so much I don't want to go back to cold Chicago?

Her foot would be better, and she might find work down there, once her foot was better.

She needed to stand on her own two feet again literally and to support herself.

She could still be Frank's girl, but she'd have more independence.

He'd really become bossy, the more homebound she'd been.

But those days were over. She was going to Miami! How she'd ever sleep, she didn't know.

"'Night, now," he said. "I'll wake you when I'm back."

She rolled onto her side, facing him. "Goodnight, Frank."

Satisfied she'd sleep like he'd told her to, he nodded and turned to leave.

Suki waited for several minutes, until she couldn't hear him and was sure he'd gone down the stairs, before she was up and out of bed again.

For goodness' sake, I can sleep on the train after I board. It's not like I'll have anyone to talk to, or anything else to do, except look out the window. I need to have my hair and makeup looking nice when it's time to go.

By the time I clean up, get dressed and get everything packed, he'll be back.

I'll just tell him I was too excited to sleep. Which is true! I'm going to Miami!

CHAPTER 6

Suki's two suitcases were loaded onto the train and the porter led her and Frank to her cabin, which Suki saw consisted of one single bed below and a window.

The porter allowed Frank on the train to help her get settled, but then Frank would have to leave, as he had no ticket.

She was in a hurry to get settled in and for him to go.

He'd been bossy from the moment he'd picked her up at her apartment, and it had begun to grate on her nerves.

The Floridian, run by the Illinois Central System, was an all-Pullman car and more luxurious than Suki had suspected.

She was grateful to Frank for the trip and trying to remain cheerful.

There would be three engine changes before she reached her destination, but she would remain in her Pullman car, as Frank told her there was no reason for her to step off the train.

He had everything all planned out and she'd listened to every detail once already, so her eyes took in the room that would be her living quarters for the next three days.

She tried to ignore the fact that Frank was repeating himself as if she were a child who hadn't gotten it right the first time.

Really, sometimes he was just too much.

"George, pay attention." Frank stowed her crutches on the overhead fold out bed after he opened it, and then he closed it again. "She won't need these until Miami."

"Yes, sir. I'll fetch them for her when it's time."

So, I'm not the only one he talks to as if he were speaking to a child. I wonder why he's calling him George. The nameplate on his porter's hat clearly says Toby.

Seeing her settled in comfortably, Frank kissed her goodbye. "Remember what I told you."

She nodded. "I'll remember."

He pressed a roll of money into the porter's hand. "See that she has anything she needs. She's to stay in her room and off that foot."

"Yes, sir. I'll take good care of Miss Suki."

"See that you do. I'll hear about it if you don't."

"Yes, sir."

He bent and kissed her one more time, said goodbye, and then he was out the door and gone.

Her compartment seemed smaller when he was standing by her bed, but once he'd gone and it was just her and the porter, it was quite roomy. The upper bunk would remain closed to give her more room and she'd enjoy the trip lounging on the bed by the window.

"Your name tag says Toby, but he kept calling you George," she said.

The porter laughed. "Yes, Miss. All porters be called George, after Mr. George Pullman." He smiled at her. "You can call me George."

She smiled back and said, "But Toby is your name, and a person should be called by their name. Why, if every porter is called George, then it's as if you're all the same." She shook her head at the idea. "That just doesn't seem right."

"Now, don't you worry over that," he said before changing the subject. "Are you comfortable enough? Can I bring you another pillow, or a blanket?"

"Yes, I'm comfortable. Thank you. Both would be nice."

He nodded and then stepped out, closing the door.

She sat gazing at the scenery, remembering what Frank wanted her to be thinking of when she looked out the window.

It made her blush. She wasn't usually a blusher, but Frank brought it out in her.

He was bold. She liked that, as she liked being bold herself.

The train started with a lurch, surprising her, and then she felt and heard the rolling of the wheels along the rails. A gentle rocking began, and she relaxed as she watched out the window, realizing she was really going to enjoy this.

What a relaxing, luxurious way to travel.

Her stomach growled.

I'm hungry, she thought. *And I'm not going to stay in this compartment when I really want to go see what else is on this train.*

He's asking too much of me.

It won't hurt to go out and get something to eat.

She got up and pulled, and pulled on the upper bed, until it opened. Then she got the crutches out.

I'll come back here and rest once I've seen what there is to see.

Leaving the upper bed open, she put a crutch under each arm and opened the door.

The porter, Toby, wasn't where she could see him, though she could hear him in another room.

She moved down the corridor, past that room, and hoped she was heading in the right direction for the dining car.

Despite what Frank thought, she wasn't going to

sit in her compartment while being waited on this whole trip.

She needed to get up and move around.

Moving slowly on her crutches as she accustomed herself to the movements of the train, she made her way.

Already this felt better, and her curiosity was being satisfied.

A uniformed waiter opened the door for her and held it while she made her way into the car.

As she entered the dining car, she took in the green velvet upholstery and the shining surfaces of brass and silverware.

The waiter pulled out her chair and seated her at a table for two, covered with fine white linen. The vase on the table held one single red rose and a spray of white baby's breath. He unfolded and placed her napkin in her lap and then handed her a menu.

"Thank you." She took the menu from him and smiled up at him. "My throat is a little bit scratchy. I'll take tea with honey to start with."

"Just the thing for a scratchy throat." He nodded his approval and then moved to the kitchen area to prepare a hot cup of tea.

She glanced over the menu and then looked outside the window at the passing scenery.

Frank's directions came back to her. *I*
'm not going to think about that.

First, she needed tea, along with a good hot meal, and then to explore her surroundings.

It was bad enough being confined in my apartment. I'm not going to be confined on this train when I've never been on one. There's too much to see and do, especially the first day. I can rest tomorrow.

The waiter returned with her tea, placing the teacup and saucer in front of her. "Are you ready to order?"

She turned back to the menu. "Yes. I want soft foods, so I'll have the baked lake trout with herbs, the au gratin potatoes, skip the salad and appetizers, and for dessert, the ice cream and cake." She looked at him. "What kind is it?"

"Chocolate cake, Miss, and vanilla or chocolate ice cream."

"Oh, that's swell. Chocolate and chocolate. Yes, I'll have that."

I'll enjoy my meal, and when I'm done maybe then I'll follow Frank's directions, because that might be fun and, well, I do have three days to entertain myself on this train. Might as well enjoy everything.

In fact, cake and ice cream every night would be more than swell.

Suki had just begun to enjoy her fish when a tall, dark, exotically handsome man with slightly olive skin entered the dining car and looked about, his brown eyes lively and intense.

His face fell.

Suki watched him.

What could've disappointed him?

He and the waiter held a conversation in lowered voices, which made her wonder even more.

They both looked at her, his intense brown eyes making her feel warm beneath his gaze.

She couldn't tear her gaze away as something in his eyes drew her to him.

The waiter said, "I will ask." Then he approached her table. "Excuse me, Miss, but there is a gentleman lacking a place to dine and he wonders if he might share your table."

"Oh, why yes, of course," she said. "He's quite welcome."

The waiter went back to speak to the man and then ushered him to the table, pulled out his seat, and waited for him to sit.

The tall gentleman sent a smile down to her and said, "Thank you for allowing me to join you. I prefer to eat in the dining car and, at this time, it seems everyone else does, too."

Oh, but he is handsome, and his voice is so nice.

His manner and way of speaking spoke of old-world manners and money.

She was delighted he'd been seated with her.

She said, "We're all hungry, and it's cold outside, so I suppose many have come in for warm beverages, and perhaps some company. It's perfectly fine to share, in such circumstances. We can pass the time more socially than dining alone."

Her words came out faster than usual, and she realized she was beginning to ramble. It must be her nerves. She was also speaking more formally.

He was no gangster, nor was he using any slang. His manner brought out a more formal manner in her.

He and Frank were as different as night and day.

"Still, I thank you. It was gracious of you to say yes."

Gracious wasn't a word anyone had ever used to describe her.

She felt uplifted hearing it, and sat a little taller.

He thinks I'm gracious. She smiled, happy at that.

He smiled back, and his smile lit her spirit like a balloon.

The waiter placed the napkin in his lap and then handed him a menu.

"Thank you, but I believe I will have what the lady is having." He handed the menu back. "And coffee. Black with two sugars."

"Very good, sir." The waiter took the menu back and went to get his coffee.

"Allow me to introduce myself. I'm Phillip Garcia." He held his hand out.

She placed her hand in his.

Oddly, her hand felt as if it belonged there, and

everything about him made her want to smile deep and long.

Every one of her senses had come alive.

Oh, this could not be, this attraction. No, no.

Can't do this right now.

He could only be a friend.

"I'm Suki." She pulled her hand back from his warmth and placed it back in her lap, safely away from him.

Her skin still felt the contact of his touch and missed it.

Oh, no. I can't be having this reaction to a stranger on the train.

No other men. Rule one. Behave, behave.

This shouldn't be so hard. Why is it?

Behave now.

She forced her thoughts under control and wished her body would follow her orders as easily.

"Just Suki?"

"Yes," she smiled. "Just Suki."

He gave her a slow, sexy smile, which made something inside her want to curl and purr. "Ah, a woman of mystery. So intriguing."

She merely smiled in return, as she tried not to let his voice creep in and put her in a state of arousal.

Not about to give a stranger on a train too much information about her, no matter how handsome he was, or how attracted she was to him, she let the smile speak for her.

Remaining silent, she tried to ignore her body's reaction to the polite, mannerly gentleman.

It was a good thing she hadn't been imagining those sexy images Frank wanted her to think of while she looked out the window when Phillip showed up. Or she would've been in deep, deep trouble.

No other men. That was rule number one.

She was breaking it already, before she'd even been on the train a full day.

Stay in your room. That was rule number two.

She was also breaking that one.

Frank wouldn't be happy.

But Frank isn't here and will never know.

She'd have three days before she was at the hotel, where his man Enzo would be guarding her.

Enzo, the warden.

She couldn't help but think of him that way. Yeah, he was there to protect her, but also to keep an eye on her and anything she might do.

Frank wouldn't hear about this time on the train.

For now, I have three days free and clear to myself, and a train to enjoy. So, I'm going to enjoy it.

"So, just Suki, where are you from?"

"Chicago." She took another bite and focused on her food.

"I should've guessed. You have that midwestern accent."

"Yes. And where are you from, Phillip?"

Pleasant conversation, she told herself. *That's all we're doing. After a nice meal I'll go back to my room, and rest. Alone.*

Keep him talking. Behave. Behave.

"Barcelona, Spain, originally. Now, Miami."

Her eyes widened, and she paused with her fork in the air. "Barcelona. How fascinating. I've never been to Barcelona. Or Miami."

"You would enjoy both."

"I'm sure."

The waiter brought Phillip's food and they ceased talking.

Suki watched his long fingers as he cut his fish precisely and took a bite. From the way he dressed and ate, even the way he carried himself, she could tell he was a gentleman.

She waited until he'd eaten a few bites and then asked, "What do you do for a living, Phillip?"

"I'm in the import and export business."

"How interesting. Do you ship things back and forth from Spain to the United States?"

"Yes." He smiled. "I do. Now, 'just Suki', tell me what you do."

"I'm a dancer. In Chicago," Suki said.

Phillip raised an eyebrow. "A dancer with a broken foot?"

His gaze settled on hers with an understanding and concern not usual in a stranger.

Oddly, he didn't seem like a stranger at all.

Yet they had only just met.

"How sad that must be for you."

He'd nailed it. A dancer who couldn't dance. It was one of the saddest things she knew.

To be unable to do what you loved. It was an immeasurable sadness.

When he looked into her eyes, he looked deeply.

How can he see me so well, to see what no one else sees?

"Yes." She looked down at her plate, and toyed with her potatoes. "It is."

"Like a painter who cannot paint, or a writer who cannot write. You must create in some way. What do you do, while you're not dancing, and waiting for your foot to heal?"

"I..." She hesitated, thinking.

Of things she hadn't thought of before.

I've been doing nothing but Frank. All day and all evening. Doing Frank. Waiting for him, pleasing him, dining with him, bathing with him, and then pleasing him again.

Having another glass of rum and then waiting for Frank.

That was her day, every day for the last four weeks. And her evening, too.

She could hardly tell Phillip that. Or even hint at it.

Her face was now beet-red.

"I don't do much," she said. "Rest, mostly. I miss dancing."

"How did you injure your foot?"

"I fell down some stairs and broke it. It was an accident." She hurried to say that last part, as from the look in his eyes she could tell he thought someone had hurt her.

Though she knew from listening to her mother, that it was what women always said. 'It was an accident.' Even when it wasn't.

To say otherwise meant you'd then have to do something about it. Something that might be dangerous.

She knew many variations of that story. Her mothers, other dancers. All ended sadly.

No, she wasn't a woman who got caught up in that kind of situation.

The first time a guy even tried to hurt Suki, she'd be out the door, long gone. She'd never be like her mother, always reaching for some man, no matter what he did to her, because she couldn't be alone.

"An accident," Phillip said.

His voice held concern. Concern from a stranger. That was new.

"Yes. I wasn't looking where I was going." She felt

the need to explain. "I was running away from gunfire. Down some stairs and wasn't looking."

"I'm glad it wasn't worse. You must be more careful," he said.

"Yes. I must," she agreed, nodding.

"I hope your foot heals soon, and you're back on the dance floor again."

It really sounded like he meant it, from the tone of his voice. *Did he?*

Could it be I've finally met one of the good guys? The respectable kind who cares about other people?

Haven't met many of those in my lifetime. Girls from the wrong side of the tracks don't.

However, I'm still Frank's girl. A gangster's moll. Not exactly free.

It's too late for anything with Phillip. The timing is all wrong.

I wish I had meet him before I hurt my foot.

Everything changed after I broke it.

"Thank you. I hope so, too. I'm going to Miami to heal, until the cast can be removed."

"Excellent idea." His eyes searched hers. "I should introduce you to my sister, Phyllis. She would enjoy meeting you."

"I'd like that." She smiled. "Are you twins?"

"Then I'll be sure to make it happen." He smiled. "Yes, she's my twin. Phyllis lights up every room she enters, and like you, she loves to dance. So, you have that in common. She'll have you cheered up in no time."

She hadn't told him a thing about Frank, or that she even had a boyfriend.

Frank wouldn't want me talking about him, or Al, or any of the other men. It would probably be wise not to mention Phillip to Frank.

But it's not like I'm doing anything wrong dining with or talking to him. We're just two people on a train, passing the time.

She convinced herself, ignoring the fact Frank had given her three rules and she wasn't following either of the first two.

Because she really liked Phillip. And there was nothing wrong with having dinner with him on the train.

But she was Frank's girl, so it couldn't go anywhere. Even if Frank would never know.

After dinner, they excused themselves to go to their rooms.

Suki planned to freshen up and then go explore the other cars. So far, she'd seen her sleeping quarters and the dining car, but not the club car or the bath car.

A bath car, she mused. *Who would've thought you could take a bath on a train? I guess with enough money you can have nearly anything.*

As Suki maneuvered down the aisles in her cast,

taking everything in, she marveled at the luxury and beauty of the cars.

This truly was traveling in style.

At the bath car the porter turned her away, saying, "If you'd like a bath, Miss, it can be arranged, but the bath is occupied right now."

"Oh, I understand," she said. "I was just wanting to look around and see where everything was, in case I want one later."

"Yes, Miss," he said.

"Is there a female attendant? Bathing can be quite a challenge with this cast on." She pointed to her foot.

"No, Miss." He shook his head. "Only gentlemen are Pullman porters. We can draw your bath and stand by with warm towels."

Certainly not used to being deferred to, Suki wondered what it would be like to have servants talking to you like this all the time.

She still couldn't get over calling every porter George, as if they didn't have names of their own.

Turning to go back down the aisle, she moved along and ended in the club car, where men were congregating and talking in a hearty manner as they smoked.

She found a seat near a window and sat looking out at the passing scenery. She could not follow Frank's directions and do what he wanted her to do.

He would control every aspect of her life if she let him. Realizing this, she came to one conclusion.

I can't let him. I'll keep his rules only if and when I want to. And I need to let him know that, so there will be no misunderstandings.

I'll find a way to tell him after he's in Miami.

Placing a slim cigarette in her cigarette holder, Suki let the club car attendant light her ciggy for her and then turned to watch out the window again. Though content to smoke with the men, or to enter any establishment that allowed her in, she noted the absence of other females in the car.

Silly of them to stay in their rooms, when they could have the freedom of sitting here just like this, she thought as she took another drag on her ciggy and blew the smoke out in a ring to amuse herself.

So busy being ladylike, they miss out on all the fun. You'd never catch a flapper doing that.

Does Frank not realize I'm a flapper and you can't pin a flapper down? He must not.

After a bit, feeling eyes upon her back, Suki turned to look where the feeling might be coming from.

A man ducked his head.

She couldn't see beneath his hat as he held his newspaper up to read it. Had he been staring at her?

He had a red scar across his right hand, as if he'd been burned.

Suki didn't like the look of him. Something

about him gave her the heebie jeebies, and she hadn't even seen his face. That alone scared her.

Suki wasn't superstitious. Her mother was a woman of the world.

Love the life you've got, because it's all you get. That's what her mother would have said.

The most spiritual things that happened to Suki were in the head rush of a good dance, or a heavy kiss.

But this guy. That scar. It sat there; staring at her like an angry spider would stare at a fly. The longer Suki looked at it, the more scared she became.

How did it happen? Was it an innocent story? Did a lamp fall on him in his sleep when he was a child? Did the scar signal disaster or danger?

Did it happen only eight months ago, after he'd already proven himself to terrible people?

Had he killed? Tortured? Was that scar from a bullet, or a branding iron?

Suki shook her head to clear it. Then she rose to go back to her room, gathering her crutches.

The man didn't raise his gaze to look at her as she left the club car.

She tossed the feeling aside as her overactive imagination and a need for sleep. But she still shivered, and the image of his scar lingered in her mind as she hobbled down the hallway.

Back in her compartment, she changed out of her traveling clothes into a pair of silk pajamas. Soft, slippery, and roomy, they were perfect to sleep in on the train. She slid beneath the covers and let the rocking of the trains wheels across the tracks be the lulling motion and lullaby, which put her to sleep.

***

Breakfast was served in her room. She ate in bed while watching the passing scenery. Feeling quite pampered, she thanked her porter. "Thank you for taking such good care of me, Toby," she said.

"You're welcome, Miss."

Finishing her breakfast, she waited for Toby to remove her tray. Then she rose, washed up, and put her makeup on. Restless, she decided to go back to the club car.

Making her way to the club car to smoke, she passed Philip and they both paused.

"Good morning," he said. "Did you sleep well?"

"It is, and I did. Slept like a baby."

"I enjoy traveling by train, for that very reason," he said. "I sleep better. Nights at sea are the same."

"It sounds lonely," she said.

"It is. Are you going to breakfast?"

"No, I've just finished breakfast and am going for a smoke."

"Very good. Perhaps you will join me for lunch later?"

"I would love to." She smiled up at him.

He smiled in return. "Half past noon good for you?"

"Yes." She nodded. "I'll meet you in the dining room."

"I'll reserve us a table."

She nodded and moved on to her compartment. There was nothing to do, she'd brought no reading material or anything to entertain herself with. She wished she'd brought a book or a magazine with her.

Well, she'd just have to settle for a nap.

THE PORTER WOKE her at noon, just as she'd asked, and brought her a cup of tea. Sipping it she looked out the window, wondering where they were now.

Perhaps Phillip would know.

After finishing her tea, she freshened her face with the water and a towel the porter had left her, then left her compartment and moved toward the dining car.

Phillip was there early, waiting, and he rose as she made her way to the table.

Their waiter seated her and placed her napkin on her lap. "Thank you," she said.

"My pleasure, Miss. What would you like to drink?"

"Tea, please," she said.

"With honey?" He asked.

"Yes."

"Of course," the waiter said.

It was what she'd ordered with her dinner last night and he had remembered.

"I'm glad you agreed to join me for lunch," Phillip said. "It makes the trip much more enjoyable, dining with you."

"Oh, I agree," she said. "Ever so enjoyable."

The waiter brought her tea and handed them their menus.

Both ordered the clam broth for an appetizer, followed by baked ham, with carrots and peas for a side, along with walnut bread, and caramel custard for dessert.

"The food has been marvelous so far," she said.

"Fine dining is always a pleasure," Phillip said.

"Yes, it is," she agreed. "I haven't been out to eat in four weeks, so this is a real treat."

"Why haven't you been out? Have you been ill other than your foot?"

"Oh, no. I'm fine otherwise. Just have this cast. But I live in an apartment, which is on the second floor with stairs, and no other way to get in or out. I couldn't manage them with this cast and these crutches."

"I see. And how did you manage to get out to come board the train?"

"I had to be carried."

His eyes searched hers. "I gather you're not married or engaged, as you're not wearing a ring."

"Nope. Not married or engaged."

Phillip nodded but didn't ask more.

And she didn't volunteer that she had a boyfriend. "And you? No wedding ring, but are you engaged?"

"I was. She decided to sleep with two other men. My cousins. I left them to fight over her, and told her to keep the ring. "

"Generous of you."

"No, not generous. I didn't want anything more to do with her. What would I do with that ring?" He shrugged.

Their soup came, and he clearly was relieved and ready to change the subject.

"Oh, that looks good," she said as she reached for her spoon. "I'm hoping you'll tell me more about Miami, since I've never been and you live there now."

"Gladly." He gave her a wide smile and then began by describing his new house and grounds and the many plants, which grew in Miami but did not grow in Chicago. His groundskeeper had just finished renovating the garden and grounds.

The rest of their lunch went smoothly, with Suki asking many questions about Phillip and Miami.

"May I enquire as to where you are staying in Miami?" Phillip asked. "So that I may call upon you?

I will bring my sister," he added before she had a chance to answer him.

"I, I really don't know," she said. "There's a driver to meet me at the station and take me and my bags to the hotel. It's all been arranged, you see."

"I do see," he said, without asking who had made the arrangements.

Dessert was served, and she suddenly realized their lunch was almost over.

"I can just picture it all, you've described it so well." She paused with her dessert spoon in her hand. "I'd never know you weren't American. Your English is perfect."

"I had an American tutor," he said, "and I speak four languages."

"Four? Oh, my. I only speak English." She tipped her head. "What are they?"

"Spanish, English, French, and Portuguese."

"They must come in handy with your import-export business."

"Yes, they do." He smiled.

"I can't imagine learning so many."

"If you learn to read Latin, it is easier. All of these are Latin-based languages."

"I didn't learn that in school. And I missed too many days taking care of my mother."

"Your mother was ill?"

"In a way, yes."

"I hope she is recovered now."

"She's fine. She lives in Chicago with her fifth husband."

He raised an eyebrow.

"My father was a boxer and a trainer. He was killed one night in an alley. I think he was murdered. But I was too young to know much, or to remember. I was only three."

"That's very young to lose a father." His warm hand closed over hers. "I'm sorry this happened to you."

"Thank you. Yes, that is too young. I don't really remember him much. They say I have his blue eyes and his black hair. He was Irish."

"Beautiful eyes." His gaze held hers in a safe, loving place. "Lovely hair."

"Thank you." She dropped her gaze, unable to face what was happening between them.

This couldn't be. The timing is wrong. Because of Frank.

"Finish your custard," he said, "and then I will walk you back to your room."

Smiling, she took her spoon for another bite.

He thinks my eyes are beautiful, and his hand is so warm and strong, yet gentle.

But I can't be falling for Phillip. I'm already Frank's girl. I can't do this.

Frank has been good to me. It wouldn't be right to fall into an affair on this very train, when Frank paid for the ticket. I won't fall.

I'm not man-crazy like my mother. Likely her man-craziness got my father killed, though they couldn't prove it.

Phillip and Suki ate quietly.

It might have been awkward, but somehow it wasn't.

He had a calm, reassuring presence and placed no pressure on her.

It was more as if he'd simply handed her the compliment and then was content to enjoy her company.

No pressure to get something in return from her. He wanted nothing from her.

"Thank you for joining me for lunch," he said. "It's made this trip much more enjoyable."

"It has. Thank you for inviting me."

"My pleasure." He gave a nod and then rose.

She stood, and he handed her the crutches.

Placing them under her arms, she began the walk back to her room.

He followed behind her, only moving forward to open and hold doors. Then they were at her room and he was standing in the doorway.

In a different time, she would have tipped her head back in hopes he would kiss her. Her gaze went to his lips automatically at the thought and she caught herself and turned her head. "Good afternoon," she said. "Thank you for escorting me."

"My pleasure." He hesitated, watching her, and then he said, "Breakfast tomorrow?"

"I believe I'll sleep in."

He dipped his head. "Of course. Then I bid you adieu, and wish you good afternoon."

The moment he was gone, and the door closed, she sank onto the bed.

Of all the luck. Why couldn't I have met him before I met Frank?

She made herself comfortable on the bed and watched the scenery roll past the window.

She'd broken rule number one, rule number two, and had yet to attempt rule number three.

The porter knocked on the door. "Come in," she said.

"Do you need anything, Miss Suki?"

"Yes, I'd like to send a telegram. You listed that as one of the services?"

"Yes, Miss."

"I'll send a telegram to Frank, and let him know I'm missing him."

"Yes, Miss." He took out a pencil and paper.

Frank's telegram would read: *Love the train. Thank you for the adventure. Miss you. Love, your Suki*

Once the telegram was sent, she felt less guilty. She told herself that, so far, she hadn't done anything wrong.

Guilt wasn't an emotion she was used to, and she didn't like it.

One of the pluses of being independent was that there was less to feel guilty about.

If you never agreed to anything, there wasn't any reason to feel guilty.

She and Frank needed to have a talk after he got to Miami. There were things that need to be ironed out. Though he wouldn't like some of them.

In the meantime, I'd better stop dining with Phillip. It will be far too easy to get into big trouble if I keep seeing him.

I will try to stay in my room and not go out again.

THE PORTER KNOCKED on her door, and then opened it, when she said, "Enter."

"We'll be stopping at Union Station for an hour and a half, Miss. But I'll be right here if you need anything."

She sat up, excited. "Oh, good." She clasped her hands. "Is it a big station? I can get out and stretch my legs."

"Mr. Frank, he wanted you to stay put."

"Well, he's not going to know. I'm certainly not telling him."

"Yes, Miss."

"Anyway, he's not here."

"Sometimes these men got eyes where you don't know it."

She thought of the man in the club car.

What if he already reported me dining with Phillip? I could be in trouble already.

Facing the porter, she said, "If he's put a tail on me, then I'm done with him. Is there one? I shouldn't have to put up with that."

"No, Miss. Not that I know of."

"Good. Now, don't worry. It will be fine and so will I."

The train would be at Jacksonville Station for little more than an hour and a half while the engines were switched, and repairs were made. Suki could step off the train to grab a bite to eat and to see as much as she could see.

She'd been in her compartment long enough, as she hadn't left it since lunch with Phillip. She didn't want to take any more meals in her room.

Getting off the train, she shuffled for the station terminal, a large building with people hurrying in and out of it. The crowd surged and heaved around her, a mass of humanity that swirled like water in an eddy.

A man in a rush passed by, so close they bumped shoulders.

Thrown off balance, Suki caught herself on the ground with her hand and left knee. "Hey!"

But the man was already gone.

"Jerk," she mumbled as she struggled to stand again.

As she raised her head, she saw the man who'd given her the heebie jeebies in the club car.

He gestured with his scarred right hand to someone behind her.

Something about him seemed off and she didn't like the look in his eyes, even though he wasn't looking at her.

Suki turned to see where he'd gestured but didn't like turning her back to him. It felt creepy, as if his gaze was strong on her back.

Whoever he'd gestured to was now lost in the crowd milling about and she couldn't find them.

She had a headache now. The pain of her ankle, the stifling mass and noise of the crowd, and the sudden Florida heat was getting to her. Even without strange, scarred men, Suki was getting stressed.

As she moved slowly on her crutches, people hurried by her on their way to catch trains. Suki hurried into the huge train station terminal building to look for a place to purchase some headache powder.

Seeing a drug store, she headed for it.

Inside, she selected headache powder, some minty gum, a new nail file, and a magazine to read. Each time Suki moved over to a new aisle, the feeling someone was watching her remained, but as soon as she turned to look over her shoulder no one was looking.

Finally, she went to the counter to pay.

Back in the main bustle of the terminal, the people moved about. Most of them seemed in a hurry to go to or from somewhere.

Her stomach growled.

Deciding to eat, she went to the restaurant and then waited for a table. Finally, one opened and she was seated and ordering.

"Tea and a slice of apple pie," she said.

That was meal enough for her and the pies in the glass case looked good.

"Sweet or unsweet?"

"What?"

The waitress smiled at her. "Iced tea, right? Do you want sugar?"

Suki stared at her in bewilderment. *Iced tea?*

Shaking her head, Suki said, "No, hot tea, please."

The waitress scribbled down her order and scurried off, leaving Suki to stare at other diners until the woman was back with a slice of pie and a cup of tea.

As Suki enjoyed her pie, she watched the people in the restaurant. Many of them were drinking some sort of auburn drink with ice.

No one was watching her, so she relaxed and forgot about the man with the scar, wondering what cold tea tasted like.

I was being paranoid, Suki thought. *It's all these people and being in a new place where I don't know anyone. This is the first time I've left Chicago, so I'm bound to be a little bit nervous. But the pie is lovely and it's fascinating watching all the people. What an adventure!*

I'm glad I didn't stay on the train. With over an hour for repairs, I'd go out of my mind just sitting in my little compartment. When it's nice, it's cozy, but when it's not, it's too small and confined.

Frank would have me never leaving my room, no matter where I'm staying, if he had his way.

Well, I can't let him have his way all the time.

And I'm having fun now.

Finishing her pie, Suki paid her bill and left a tip. Deciding to go back to her compartment to rest, she rose to go. It was too smoky in here anyway, and she'd forgotten her cigs back in her smaller carry bag. Her evening bag with all her money was all she'd brought with her.

Suki wondered where Phillip was right now and how he was occupying his time. It was too bad she had to travel alone.

She didn't like dining alone. Phillip was pleasant company and Suki hadn't had a real conversation with anyone but Frank or Tessa since she'd hurt her foot.

She was starving for social interaction, not food. Maybe Phillip would join her for another meal. They would just have to behave themselves.

Suki headed for the newspaper stand to buy another magazine to read on the train. Just as she was perusing them, the feeling someone was watching her returned. This time she didn't look but brushed it off, attributing it to her nerves and imagination.

She purchased two more magazines and then headed back, stopping on the way to purchase a single red rose from the florist. The rose was a fragrant one and she enjoyed its scent.

Breathing in, she told herself, *A woman should buy herself flowers and never wait for a man to do it.*

Her experience with flowers was that a man only sent them when he'd done something wrong and wanted to make up for it. Her mother used to fall for that one, but Suki never would. The one guy who'd tried, she'd refused to answer the door to. And that had been the end of that, and him.

When Suki was done with a man, she was done.

Her mind was on all this as she approached the train, and not on her surroundings.

Hearing footsteps fast-approaching behind her, she turned.

A large, swarthy man in a black coat had hurried up to her, and was reaching out to grab hold of her with both his hands, just as Suki turned and saw him.

Her right hand brought her crutch slightly forward before slamming it backwards, right up between his legs.

The man cried out in agony and fell, clutching himself.

Getting her balance back, Suki hurried toward the train with a run-hop, using her crutches to lean on while alternating hopping on her good foot.

She run-hopped toward the steps of the train and the porter reached his hand out to her from inside the train. "You all right, Miss?"

"Yes," Suki panted, out of breath as she looked over her shoulder to see if the man had followed. "I am now."

The man who'd tried to grab her was still on his side on the pavement.

Suki thought she saw him tremble, and she nodded in satisfaction.

Phillip, who'd seen what had happened from the other end of the platform, where he'd finished conducting business with a courier, hurried up to where she was boarding.

Looking back to where the man had fallen, he spoke to Suki.

She heard him speak low as his words traveled through the evening, just three soft words reaching her. "*Cuidado, mi Amor*."

She nodded, not understanding him, wanting only to be inside, safe inside her compartment again.

Though Suki had no clue as to their meaning, his words stored in the back of her mind for later, as she moved inside toward her warm, safe bed.

Once inside, she pulled off her coat and thrust her crutches into the corner, sick of them. Though it was a good thing she'd had them.

Who knew a crutch could make such a good weapon? I whacked him good.

Then the shock of what had just happened, and what had nearly happened, hit her and made her feel cold and shaky.

She curled beneath the blankets, and when Toby popped his head in to check on her, she ordered a cup of hot tea and another piece of chocolate cake.

When he returned, he'd managed to not only bring her the tea and chocolate cake, but chocolate ice cream as well.

"Oh, thank you," she said.

"Yes, Miss," he said. "A scare like that, you need extra chocolate." He gave her a wink.

"I appreciate it," she said. "Looks delicious."

"Enjoy. Ring when you're done, and I'll remove the tray."

She heard Phillip and Toby talking outside her room as Phillip inquired how she was and if she was okay. He told Toby to let him know if she needed anything. Any time, night or day.

That was nice of him. It's nice to have someone to watch over me.

The tea and the chocolate did much to calm her nerves, as well as knowing Phillip wasn't far if anything went wrong.

Soon she was warm and relaxed again, curled beneath a blanket after ringing for Toby to come remove the tray.

As the train rolled down the line she watched out her window, showing her the scenery moving by, and she thought of Frank, wishing he were here to wrap her into his strong, warm arms and make love to her, remembering the night he had saved her life and taken her home.

Phillip, who was passing her doorway again, paused listening for her, and then continued to the drawing room where the men smoked cigars.

She's quite a woman. Bravely fighting off a large man with her crutches instead of screaming and letting the man grab her. Now the lady wants to be alone.

Too bad she doesn't want company. 'Just Suki' was a fascinating woman. Worthy of a good man.

I must learn more of her when we are in Miami. And I must discover what her secrets are and who might wish to harm her. So that I might keep her safe. In the meantime, I'll keep an eye on the feisty beauty so nothing else befalls her.

Suki fell asleep to the rocking of the train wheels over the tracks and slept soundly without bad dreams, despite the man almost grabbing her.

She remembered the bad dream she'd had right after the shoot-out at the club when Frank had held her after she woke in the night, crying out. He had been good to her then, comforting her, making her feel safe, and the bad dream had not returned.

This time when she dreamed, instead of a bad dream, she dreamed of men coming at her one and her swinging her crutch at them, making them stop.

"*Cuidado, Mi Amor*," Phillip said, then he kissed her hand and led her into a grand ballroom. Suddenly she was dancing, the cast gone, and she went into one spin after another, feeling free.

All she'd ever wanted was to be free.

In the dream she was free and spinning around and around in celebration of that feeling with Phillip right beside her.

In Miami at the busy station, a large brooding man wearing a dark coat and hat stepped forward the minute Suki went to step off the train.

"Frank sent me to collect ya," he said, as he reached for her.

Drawing back quickly with her crutch, which made him frown, was a reaction from her having been almost nabbed at the Jackson station.

She frowned back at him and asked, "How do I know Frank sent you? What's your name?"

"Enzo. He give you my name?"

"Yes." Giving a huge sigh of relief, her frown disappeared. "Good. Can't be too careful." She spoke low and didn't mention her earlier adventure.

Enzo gave a nod. "Dame like you has to be careful. That's good." His tone was gruff but showed approval. "Frank sent me to look after ya." He reached for her again. "Come on, you're holding everyone up."

"Oh, yes. Sorry." She let him help her down, and the porter collected her two bags and gave them to Enzo.

"It ain't far to the car," he said as he picked her suitcases up. "If ya think ya can walk it."

"I don't mind a walk. I don't get enough exercise these days."

"Frank wants ya resting at the hotel. I'll take ya anywhere ya need to go and bring ya whatever ya need if the hotel don't have it."

"Thank you."

"No problem, doll. We take care of our own."

"Yes, Frank's been good to me."

He grunted as if to say 'of course' and moved ahead of her, carrying the bags.

His gaze was constantly scanning from left to right and back again.

What is he looking for? Or who?

Once they were in the car headed for the hotel, she asked him, "Who were you looking for at the station? I got this way when three guys shot up the Green Mill in Chicago."

"Yeah, I heard about that. Sorry about your foot, but broke foot is better than dead."

"Much better, you're right. And thank you. Frank rescued me and that's how we ended up together. Did they ever catch those guys?"

"Nah. Northsiders shot up Al's car second week of January and then twelve days later tried to kill Torrio outside his house. Then four days later these three guys they shipped in shot up the club. Al's got everyone watching real close, now. Like I said, we take care of our own. You'll be safe with me. It ain't safe to go anywhere by yourself and Frank don't want that anyhow. So, you call me, I come get ya and ya can go wherever ya want."

"I appreciate you driving me around. I've got two more weeks in this cast, or more like a week and a half 'cause it was two when I got on the train. Then I'll be able to get around better."

"Your foot might be better then, but it still ain't safe to go by yourself. An' Frank don't want that. You just don't worry about it. Pick up the phone. I'll bring the car and pick ya up."

"Okay. I'll call if I need anything. Thank you."

He simply grunted in return.

The rest of the ride was silent. Enzo wasn't much of a talker. She supposed part of his job was to be quiet and pay attention. It could mean life or death if he wasn't paying attention. The shooting at the club had taught her that.

The Flamingo Hotel had only been open five years and, as the first grand hotel in Miami, it was established as the place to be. Everything was still new and glamorous.

As they pulled onto the grounds Suki's eyes widened. The space was enormous.

Phillip had told her there were tennis courts, volleyball, a pool with cabanas and palm trees and a sand beach; there was boating, as well as an outdoor tea garden and a golf course.

But he'd neglected to tell her there was an elephant!

Hardly able to believe her eyes, she rolled the car window down and watched as an elephant paraded a covered wagon down the street. The wagon was filled with laughing adults and children.

Enzo drove slowly past them, so she could look her fill.

Once they were past, she turned to Enzo. "Can you believe they have an elephant? At a hotel! That's amazing!"

Enzo said, "Yeah, I seen it before." Looking all around, he then drove the car up to the front of the hotel and parked. "Sit tight while I get the bags."

She waited while he unloaded her bags and gave them to the uniformed bellman, who handed them off to another uniformed man to carry in.

Enzo came and opened the car door and helped her out.

Putting the crutches under her arms, she said, "I hope there aren't a lot of stairs."

"No stairs for you," he said.

One of the hotel employees hurried up to them with a wheelchair.

"You're kidding, right?" She couldn't believe it. She'd done without a wheelchair for four weeks and didn't need one now.

"No joke. Sit down," Enzo said. "Frank don't want ya on that foot."

With a sigh, she sat and was wheeled into the lobby of the hotel and over to the concierge's desk. The hotel register was brought over to the desk for her to sign and everyone was fussing over her.

She found it all a bit silly, as she could've stood at the counter like anyone else and signed.

Frank must've made me sound like an invalid. Just wait till I get this cast off. I'll show you Frank Omato, that I'm no invalid. Once I'm on the dance floor again.

There was a telegram waiting for her from Frank.

Call. Miss you too. Love, Frank

And in her room twenty-four red roses were waiting.

It's hard to stay mad at him when he keeps doing nice things like this.

"I need to call Frank," she said.

Enzo pushed her wheelchair over to the table, which held the phone. He took paper and pen and wrote his number down. "Ya need anything ya call me at this number."

"Thank you," she said.

"All set now, before I go?" he asked. "I'll leave ya alone to talk to Frank."

"No, I'm good. See you later."

He nodded and then he went out the door and was gone.

She picked up the phone to call Frank.

When he answered, she said, "The flowers are beautiful. Thank you."

"Thought you'd like them. How's your room?"

"Bigger than I thought it would be, and there's even a balcony."

"Yeah, I figured you'd like that. Since you were complaining about no fresh air. Then being cooped up on the train with the windows closed. You can enjoy fresh air on the balcony. Plenty of fresh air in Miami and you don't even have to leave your room."

There it is, that not leaving to go anywhere part again.

The part she didn't like so much.

Still everything else is nice. More than nice, she felt like a princess here in this room, and he had everyone treating her like one.

He was spoiling her, and she liked that part very much.

"It's real pretty here. Did you know they have an elephant? We passed it coming in."

"How about that. Are you having fun?"

"Yes. That made me laugh, it was such a surprise to see an elephant walking down the street in front of this grand hotel."

"Glad you're having fun, babe. How was the train ride?"

"The food was delicious, and the rocking helped me sleep at night."

"Good. You behave yourself?"

"Frank, there's not much trouble to get into on a train. I'm glad for the balcony and the fresh air now. I think I'll go sit out there after we get off the phone."

"Good girl. I'll bring ya something pretty."

"More gifts? You spoil me, Frank."

"You're worth it, doll. Now, go enjoy your balcony. I got to go meet a guy."

"Okay, thanks, Frank."

"Dream of me and I'll be there soon. Call ya tomorrow with the time."

"Okay. 'Bye, Frank. Be careful out there."

"Don't worry, doll. 'Bye now."

Suki went out to the balcony and sat watching the palm trees wave.

Later, she ordered a sandwich and tea from room service and they served it on the balcony.

She enjoyed the sunshine and fresh air until she decided to attempt a bath, something that was never easy with a cast. She ended up keeping the water level low in the tub and propping her cast up on the side. But at least she had nice warm water, lovely scented soap, and a soft fluffy towel. After spot-washing on the train, it felt wonderful. Using a cup from the ice tray, she was able to wash and rinse her hair.

By the time she was out and toweled off, it had taken her a whole hour to take a bath.

Still wearing the towel, she decided to sit on the balcony and let her hair dry in the fresh air.

This feels positively decadent and wonderful. Florida is like paradise. I could stay here and never go back to cold Chicago.

CHAPTER 7

*S*uki lay in her hotel bed, smoking, and blowing smoke rings at the ceiling. The truth was, she only smoked when she was out with other people, or when she was bored. If she stayed active enough she didn't smoke at all, though if a man offered her a ciggy she always accepted. It was a part of the flapper lifestyle, though one she could take or leave.

Her consumption of rum was quite another story. Quite simply, she loved the taste and the way it made her feel, compared to the way she felt when she hadn't been drinking. With her foot hurting constantly, she'd gone with the alternative, which was to keep a continual buzz going.

This wasn't a problem, as Frank kept her supplied with hooch. Any kind of hooch she wanted.

He was always filling up her glass and making sure the silver flask he'd given her was never empty.

Now she was bored and out of hooch. Here in Miami, she didn't know how to get ahold of any.

Crossing one bent leg over the other she circled her good foot around and around, wishing she could exercise the other one.

All this staying still, and not being able to go and do, to go and do whatever I want, is enough to drive me mad.

Should've thought to ask Frank how to get more rum when he called. Too late now.

Maybe Enzo will know.

The front desk delivered a message to Suki, which interrupted her thoughts.

The message was from Phillip.

It read: *Ready for some fresh air? Lunch tomorrow eleven-thirty at The Flamingo Hotel Tea Garden. Phyllis is looking forward to meeting you.*

Oh, how lovely, she thought.

Taking a pen and paper she wrote: *Can't wait to meet her. Looking forward to seeing you both tomorrow.*

She called down to the front desk to have the message delivered. She couldn't wait to go to lunch with Phillip again, and to meet his sister, Phyllis.

THE NEXT DAY, she was faced with the dilemma of what to wear to their lunch. Sorting through her clothes, she picked one of her old flapper dresses.

She tugged it over her head and tried to pull it down over her breasts.

Oh, no. I've gained too much weight. It's all this sitting around, eating. And lounging in silk pajamas and silk nightgowns, waiting for Frank.

All this sitting around, waiting on a man.

Well, I've had enough of that! No more sitting around and waiting any more. For anyone.

Never again.

Tugging the too-snug dress off again, she opted for a pair of silk pajamas. Black, with pale pink roses, an Oriental look.

Eyeing herself in the mirror, she said, "Well. I'll simply start a new trend of wearing silk pajamas to luncheons. Women do wear trousers now. In fact, we wear whatever we please. And this is what I please."

Putting a diamond-covered barrette in one side of her black hair, she pulled it up, showing off her pink and diamond earrings. They were a gift from Frank the week before he took her to the train station. With a retouch of her lipstick, she was ready.

Taking up her crutches she went to the door, opened it, and peered out.

Enzo was nowhere in sight.

Good.

She made her way to the Tea Garden, which was

outdoors beneath some palm trees. She loved watching the palms and the way they swayed with the breeze. Florida was warm and lovely; it felt like spring or early summer in Chicago.

Suki was so glad to leave the snow behind, that she'd vowed not to think of it again, unless someone brought it up.

Phyllis Garcia was a dark-haired girl with light brown skin, big brown eyes with expressive eyebrows, and full lips adorned with deep red lipstick. She stood beautifully striking next to her brother Phillip.

Suki noted how handsome he was, and how his smile made him even more handsome, as she hobbled up to them.

"Suki," he said as she drew near. "You look lovely and rested."

"It's good to see you again, Phillip," she said. "Thank you for suggesting lunch."

"It's good to see you, too,' he said. "Allow me to introduce my sister, Phyllis. Phyllis, this is Suki, my friend from the train."

"Pleased to meet you," Phyllis said. "I've heard so much about you."

"And I you," Suki said.

Then they were being led to their table, and everyone but the maître d followed along behind her, as she hobbled on her crutches.

Their waiter pulled out a chair for her, and as

she sat, he said, "May I take these for you?" Just as if they were a coat and hat and nothing so unusual as crutches.

"Why, yes," she said. She hadn't thought about where to put them at the table and there really wasn't a place for them. She couldn't be rid of them soon enough.

Handing them to the maître d, she turned back to Phillip and Phyllis, who were now seated. "I get this cast off in one more week," she said. "And I cannot wait."

"Phillip tells me you're a dancer," Phyllis said.

"Yes. I was. Until this happened."

"I, too, am a dancer." Phyllis smiled.

"You're from Spain; do you do the flamenco?" Suki asked.

"I know this dance, yes. But I am not a flamenco dancer. That takes many years of practice." Phyllis laughed. "Some say dance is the national art of Spain. Every region has its own version of dance. Flamenco is the most widely-known form of Spanish dance outside of Spain, and it was spread by the Gitano's."

"Oh, gypsies." Suki's eyes widened. "Do you know any?"

"Flamenco dancers, yes. Some are Gitano. They do not like to be called gypsies."

"I see," Suki said. "I've never heard them called Gitano before."

"Most Americans call them gypsies," Phillip said, "because they don't know any other term for them."

The waiter appeared to take their order.

"I shall have the salmon croquettes, and a leafy salad. Lemonade to drink," Phyllis said to the waiter, and then she directed her attention to Suki. "If you haven't dined here yet, you must try the croquettes. They are delicious."

"Well, then. I shall have the same." Suki nodded, and then handed her menu to the waiter. "I'll have everything she's having. It all sounds delicious."

Phillip ordered the medallion of spring lamb, and potatoes a la hollandaise, which made Suki smile.

Men did like their meat and potatoes, and it appeared Phillip was no exception.

Once their orders were taken, the waiter left, and Phyllis took charge of the conversation again.

"Now that you have a week until the cast is off, what shall we do to entertain ourselves? What games do you play? Dominoes, Yahtzee, Bunco, Parcheesi, cards? We can play poolside, and enjoy watching the handsome men in their bathing suits."

Suki laughed.

Oh, this was going to be fun.

She said, "I've played cards and Yahtzee, but never played dominoes, or Parcheesi, and never heard of Bunco."

"Then we'll start with Parcheesi, and I'll teach you the others. Did you bring a swimsuit?"

"An old one. I'll need to swim, and rehabilitate my foot, but I didn't have time to shop for a new one, and this time of year the stores in Chicago are selling sweaters, not swimsuits."

"We can go shopping for a new one, after your cast is off. I'll love to shop, and can't wait to show you all the good stores."

"That's a great idea. Thank you."

"You're welcome, my friend. I'll ring you tomorrow. We'll plan an afternoon by the pool."

Lunch with Phillip and Phyllis flew by, and was over before Suki knew it. She and Phyllis had hit it off right away, just as Phillip had predicted. She was so glad he'd suggested they meet.

They saw her to her room, and she showed them the balcony, and the view, which they all agreed was lovely.

"Now, do you need anything, before we go?" Phyllis asked.

"No, I'm good." Suki yawned. The warm Miami sun, and her full belly were making her sleepy.

"Time for siesta," Phyllis laughed. "We will be going now, so you can rest. Tomorrow we siesta in the cabana." Her eyes twinkled. "And watch for the handsome cabana boy."

Suki laughed, too.

Phyllis was so much fun.

"I can hardly wait."

"We'll see ourselves out. You go on and relax," Phyllis said.

Phillip handed her a piece of paper with a number written on it. "If you need anything, call and ask for either of us."

"Thank you for everything," Suki said. "You two are the bees knees."

"Thanks, lalapazaza," Phyllis gave her a wave, and then they went out the door.

Suki had just gotten comfortable on the bed, when the phone rang. She got up to answer the phone, thinking it might be Phyllis or Phillip again.

Maybe they'd forgotten something and were calling from downstairs.

"Hello?"

"Where you been?" Frank's voice growled into the phone.

He's spoiled, she thought.

Spoiled, because I'm always there when he calls, or stops by. Because I couldn't go anywhere before. But just because I've been living like that, it doesn't mean it's going to stay that way.

Frank might think he owns me, but he doesn't. No man owns me.

"Having lunch with Phyllis, here at the hotel. We ate at the Flamingo Hotel Tea Garden, which is sort of out on the lawn. It's nice to have fresh air, after being inside on the train, and the weather is so warm, and the sunshine feels so good."

She was babbling along, sensing his mood in the silence, and knowing he was angry and could be growing angrier. Still, she babbled along.

"Who the hell is Phyllis?" Frank growled again, interrupting her.

"She's from Spain. She and her family moved here to Miami this year. But she already knows everyone, it seems. She's a great gal. You'll like her. And she's a twin."

She was babbling again, but she couldn't help it. Sometimes Frank made her nervous.

He interrupted her again. "Hooking up with twins is Rocco's kind of deal. And I don't need our relationship mixed up with other people. If I'd wanted that, I'd have told ya."

"She's just a gal pal to have fun with. I need some female companionship. And she has a twin brother, not a sister."

"You ain't sleeping with no one but me. Not even another woman."

"Of course not, Frank. You have nothing to worry about."

"I ain't the one who'd have something to worry about." He was still growling, though he sounded as if he might be less angry now.

"I can't just sit here in my hotel room, by myself, Frank."

"Where else ya been? An' don't tell me the hotel. She lives in Miami, so she ain't stayin' in the hotel. Where'd ya meet her?"

"Oh, but I did meet her in the hotel."

That was the truth at least. Better to stick as close to that as possible.

"She was here looking at the hotel for some sort of reception."

"You went to a reception? Whose?"

"I've no idea. I didn't go. I don't even know when it is. It's still being planned. I met her in the powder room."

"Why the hell were you up on that foot? You're supposed to be resting. When I tell you to do something, I expect you to do it."

And there's the problem, she thought, frowning.

You don't own me. And I can't live like this.

This was the dilemma she was in, however. And in a new city with her foot in a cast, and no job.

Well, she would work on that, as well as getting the cast off and rehabbing her foot.

For now, she'd go along with Frank. If he kicked her out, she couldn't even go stay with a friend. Everyone she was close enough to, to flop on their couch, lived all the way back in Chicago.

"I'm out of hooch, Frank. I was downstairs looking for some."

Changing the subject might work to calm him down.

"Why the hell didn't you say so? Tell me, or Enzo. Dammit, woman, you've got no sense. You can't go wandering around the hotel, looking for hooch. Where'd you think you would find it?"

"I don't know. This is a very proper establishment. But Phyllis had a flask, and shared a bit."

"In the powder room." His flat tone told her he didn't believe her.

And he really shouldn't have, as she was making this up as they talked.

"Yes. In the powder room. I asked if she knew where to find some, and she said 'right here', and then showed me the flask on her thigh."

She was spinning the lie as fast as she could, and hoping he'd believe her. Because she wasn't going to be cut off from Phyllis, her one girlfriend in this town. They'd hit it off right away, as if they'd known each other for life.

Phyllis might be a new friend, but she was already a good one.

"Listen, doll," he interrupted again. "Behave yourself. Don't make me have to punish ya. Hang on." His voice changed as he spoke to someone in the room. "Yeah, I'm coming. Just a minute." He came back to the phone. "Gotta go. I'll see ya soon. Behave."

"I'll behave, don't worry about me, Frank. See you soon."

Less than five minutes after she hung up the phone, there was a knock on her door.

She went to open it.

Enzo stood looking at her. He said, "Frank wanted me to check on you." He moved past her, into the room, and looked around, opening all the doors, and looking behind them.

"No one here," Suki said, and gave a shrug. "Just little ole me. Nothing to see. And absolutely nothing to do."

Obviously, Frank had told Enzo to keep an eye on her. And likely had called him, when he couldn't reach her on the phone.

He'd suspected she was with another guy. Because Enzo checked her balcony, then inside her closet, and the bathroom.

Finding no bad guy lurking, and no lover hiding, Enzo grunted, and then left.

Probably to report to Frank.

She wasn't going to trust Enzo for anything. He'd likely report everything he saw, or heard, directly to Frank.

THE NEXT MORNING, someone knocked on Suki's door and when Suki went to open it, Phyllis stood there with her arms full of bags. "Good morning, lalapazaza."

"Good morning. Come on in." Suki laughed. "Are you going to call me good sport every time you see me?"

"Of course!" Phyllis laughed. "I don't know many gals who'd be cooped up in a stuffy little apartment for weeks, and not turn into an old sour puss. You're high spirited, just like me, and that's why we'll be thick as thieves, before you know it."

Suki laughed. No one lifted her spirits the way Phyllis could.

"Thank you."

"Come on, let's see which sun outfit looks best on you, and then we'll go down to the pool ,and order champagne from the cabana boy."

"They'll serve champagne?"

The hotel's formal policy was, they didn't serve alcohol.

"He'll serve the bottle I dropped off there, on my way up, or he won't get another nice tip, where the first one came from." Suki winked.

Soon they were downstairs playing Parcheesi.

All Suki knew how to play was poker, because her 'uncles' had taught her at a young age.

Sunning by the pool, on two chaise loungers, with the Parcheesi board on a table between them, they sipped champagne, and watched the other bathers.

Suki sat fanning herself, her cast growing hotter in the sun, as the day grew warmer.

"You're positively pink," Phyllis said. "Let's move into the cabana, so you can cool down. It doesn't do to burn your skin on your first day in the sun."

"I'm white as a ghost compared to you," Suki said. She reached for her crutches.

"My skin has always been olive toned," Phyllis said as she picked up her wide brimmed straw hat. "I started off with browner skin than you." She laughed. "So I will always be darker than you. I can still burn, but not as quick, and by the next day I'm tanned and brown."

"Lucky," Suki said. "Sunburn hurts. I had a bad burn one summer when I was a child, and it took weeks to heal."

Phyllis placed her hat on Suki's head. "There. You mustn't ruin your complexion in this hot Florida sun," Phyllis said. "Your skin is lovely and pale, like an angels. The contrast with your dark hair and blue eyes is stunning. Phillip is quite taken with you, and I see why. You two would make lovely children, if you were to marry. Don't you agree?"

Shocked by the direct words of her new friend, Suki was momentarily speechless.

Phillip.

The thought of being with him, and having his children, seemed an unreachable fairytale dream. Even if she were free to be with him, Phillip was out of her league, wasn't he?

Still standing, leaning on her crutches, she gazed

off across the pool, to where a man was drying off after a swim.

Without turning her head to look at Phyllis, she said, "Your brother is very nice. I enjoy his company. If I weren't already with Frank, I'd be free to spend more time with Phillip. But I'm not free." She let her words trail away, lost in the 'what if''s', and the 'could not be's'. If she and Phillip had met sooner, everything would have been different.

In a soft, understanding tone, Phyllis said, "Who is Frank?"

Suki looked around, uncomfortable talking about him out in the open.

Realizing this, Phyllis helped her into the cabana, holding the curtain.

Once they were inside, Phyllis closed the curtain.

Then Suki whispered, "Frank Omato. One of Al Capone's enforcers."

Phyllis was suddenly silent and her eyes widened.

They exchanged a glance.

A gangster's moll didn't just stop seeing the gangster. Such men were dangerous. And possessive. It wouldn't be easy to tell such a man no.

Flapper or not, it wasn't as if Suki could say, I want to see someone else, or I want to date others, or we are through.

Though she was a flapper, she was only as free as the arrangement between she and Frank allowed.

"I understand," Phyllis said. "I'll let Phillip know."

"I do like enjoy his company," Suki sighed. "I wish things weren't so complicated. Once Frank arrives, it will be hard to see the two of you."

"You do what you must do to be safe. Neither of us wants to endanger you."

"Thank you."

Phyllis placed her hand over Suki's. "We're your friends. If you need us, either of us, then come to us, or send for us, and we will help."

"That's good to know," Suki said. "Thank you."

"Now," Phyllis pulled the curtain back, and gestured to the cabana boy. "More champagne!"

It turned out there really was a reception, and Phyllis really was attending. Suki couldn't have guessed any better.

The only thing was, Phyllis hadn't been involved in setting up the reception. She was just a guest.

Suki was glad of the reception, though, because Frank was likely to check on her, using Enzo, and now there really was a reception for Suki to go to.

It was a miracle Enzo had been nowhere around when Suki and Phyllis chatted over lunch by the pool.

He'd shown up, glowering just as they were

making their way back to Suki's room. He'd glowered the whole time he followed them there, and as soon as Phyllis left, he'd told Suki that she wasn't to even go down to the pool, without telling him.

Suki just nodded, went inside her room, and closed the door.

Tonight, they were all going to have drinks at the private reception in the hotel. Friends of Phillip and Phyllis were celebrating their engagement this evening.

Suki bathed, and then put on her makeup.

Sitting on the balcony in her robe, her hair dried quickly. Had anyone been watching, it would appear she was in for the evening.

After a while, she went back inside and dressed quickly. Then she headed for the reception.

Suki entered the ballroom and scanned the room, looking for Phillip or Phyllis. She spotted Phyllis not far from the Champagne tower. She made her way over to her.

Phyllis wore deep red lipstick, and a black shawl embroidered with red roses, over a black sequined flapper dress.

"How lovely," Suki said, touching the shawl. "Spanish?"

"*Si*," Phyllis said, "from Barcelona."

Introductions went around, and Suki met Arnie, Phyllis's escort. He was tall and extremely thin.

"We just returned, for an engagement and wedding." Arnie laughed, reading Suki's expression.

"Yours?" she asked, wondering if that meant he was engaged to Phyllis, and what he was laughing about.

He was making no sense to her.

"No, not ours." He shook his head, amused at the idea.

Phyllis, Suki noted, was taking his reaction in. Then she rolled one shoulder, as if she hadn't a care in the world and blithely said, "Be a dear, and fetch me another glass of champagne, darling."

Arnie nodded. "Of course, doll."

Giving his attention to Suki, Phillip said, "Two glasses?"

"Of course," Suki replied, mimicking Arnie, then tossed her head to the side, and flipped her dark bobbed hair in the air. "Always."

They all laughed.

Flappers had to have a devil may care attitude or be thought dull and Suki had that attitude down to a T.

As the men walked away, the two women looked at each other in understanding.

"He's not the type for marriage," Suki said. "He only wants to play."

"Today, I'll play," Phyllis said. "We'll see if Arnie can keep up. I've got my eye on a pair of ruby teardrop earrings. I simply must have them, or I'll be heart-broken." She laughed. "Though he's had a lot to drink, and is making little sense right now, he's a good egg."

"Those earrings would be perfect with your shawl." Suki smiled. "Interesting you should choose teardrop-shaped earrings, though." She raised an eyebrow. "Are you sure he isn't breaking your heart?"

"I won't let him." Phyllis pulled a cigarette out of her purse and placed it in a holder, then watched for him to return, to light it for her. "I simply won't let him. The earrings will remind me not to cry over any man. Even him. Once was enough."

Suki nodded, and watched the men approach with glasses of champagne.

Phillip held Suki's out to her and she took it and raised it.

Arnie handed the other glass to Phyllis, who took it and raised her glass as well.

"Here's to staying up," Suki said. "And never letting anyone, or anything, bring us down."

"Hear, hear," Phyllis and the men said, as they raised their glasses and clinked them together in a toast.

As they chatted, Suki learned more about Arnie, who liked to talk about himself.

Arnie Lewis was a businessman who also worked in fine imports, his most recent trade being Ming vases. As the wealthy poured into Miami, decorating their new homes and business offices, Mr. Lewis was quick to recognize yet another way to make money from his imports.

He'd met Phyllis at a local art showing. Fresh from Barcelona, Phyllis, with her old-world Spanish money, had caught his eye. He'd been showing her about town ever since.

"I see your friendly bodyguard is nearby," Phyllis said. "Should we offer him a drink?"

Enzo hovered just outside the reception area, which bothered Suki so much, she couldn't even look at him.

"We're not offering him anything," Suki said. "I'm sure Frank pays him enough."

"At least he's not nearby, listening to every word we say," Phyllis said.

"No, but he watches everything, and then he reports back to Frank," Suki said. "I won't have to tell him how my evening went, he'll have already heard all about it."

Phillip moved so that his back was to Enzo, and then he said, "If you want to disappear for a while, I could always put you on one of the ships sailing to Spain. I doubt any of his men would follow you there."

"You don't know Frank," she said. "He can be very possessive."

"I don't care to know Frank," he said. "I do care that you are happy."

"Thank you for that," Suki said. "It's nice to know

you care. Now how about another glass of champagne?" She held her empty glass out to him. "Keep them coming. My foot hurts, and I want to get ossified."

This was true, but mostly she wanted to forget about Enzo watching her every move.

"You should come out to our house this weekend, and see the horses," Phyllis said.

"I would love that," Suki said. "But Enzo will probably follow me."

"Don't let that stop you," Phyllis said. "It's a large place. He can come along. Don't worry about him. We will handle him."

THE WEEKEND ARRIVED, and Suki had Enzo drive her to visit Phyllis and Phillip, since he'd been hovering even more lately, and insisted on going with her whenever she left the hotel.

Slipping away alone for any length of time was impossible.

The house was a sprawling mansion in Suki's eyes, as she'd never been in a house as big as this one, with such high ceilings and chandeliers. Nor had she known anyone who had servants.

Phillip and Phylis lived on a different level than the gangsters Suki had spent time with. Theirs was old money, and they were from Spain, with old world manners.

After a quick tour of the house, they went outside for tea and sandwiches on the back lawn. From there, she could see the stables and a caretaker's house.

Phyllis had provided instructions for Enzo to be served lunch in the kitchen.

Suki thought it would be a nice break from the man, until she noticed Phillip watching the back porch and patio.

"He's there, isn't he?" she asked. "He's always there."

"He's fine. It's his job to watch you, so he's not going to sit in the kitchen. Don't let him disturb you, he's just enjoying the view," Phillip said. "Come, I'll show you the stables, and our horses."

"Oh, yes. I'd love to see them," Suki said.

She'd heard about their race horses and was excited for the chance to see them, close up.

He moved to help her out of her chair, and handed her the crutches. Moving far enough away from her that Enzo could not find fault with his movements, he waited until she was ready, and then he walked slowly toward the stables, so Suki could keep up.

She hobbled along beside him on her crutches, noting that he was aware of Enzo and giving her distance, but that he would stop and help her if she needed it, she admired the handsome man beside her.

He's always so thoughtful and mannerly.

Enjoying his presence beside her, and the attention he gave her, she smiled at him.

"I get this cast off next week."

"Excellent news." He smiled at her. "You'll be dancing again in no time."

Tired of the clunky thing, she couldn't wait to get the cast cut off next week. The heavy cast made her slow, and wore her out if she moved around too much.

It was really cramping her style, making it hard to be her energetic, bubbly self.

All this weight weighing her down was no fun at all.

She was so tired of everything weighing her down. Her cast, Enzo, Frank.

Phylis and Phillip were the only ones lifting her instead of weighing her down. Being with them, she felt more free.

At the stables he led her inside. "We'll visit Gemini first," he said. "Her sire is Capella, and her dam is Gemini. She's not running this year because she's carrying a foal. We're retired her, and won't be breeding her after this one."

Suki knew nothing about horses, but from the way he spoke, she understood what he meant.

They passed a stall, which held a sign saying, Gemini.

The horse in the stall snorted, and turned its head, from where the groomer was brushing it.

"Hey Joe, can we get Gemini out of her stall, I want to show her to Miss Suki."

"Yes, sir," Joe, a short, older man said.

He led a beautiful mare, with a sleek brown coat out.

Phillip held his hand out, palm up, and Gemini nibbled at his offering. "Hello girl, how are you today?" His tone was intimate and kind.

Listening to him made Suki's heart melt. He obviously loved this horse.

"What are you feeding her?"

"Sliced carrot. She loves sweets, but we don't give her sugar cubes. Carrot is healthier. She'll have a foal in the spring. Come, pet her. She's a gentle horse."

These horses in the stable were tall and sleek, thoroughbred racers, very different from any horses Suki had seen in Chicago, pulling wagons, or carrying mounted police.

These were larger and more intimidating.

Suki edged up, closer to Gemini, and tentatively reached out her hand.

"Go on, she won't hurt you," he said as he continued petting the horse.

Suki softly touched the side of her mane and gave a soft pat, and then pulled her hand back.

She felt too awkward on her crutches to want to do more, and used the crutches as an excuse to move back. She backed to a wall and leaned against it.

Phillip watched her and said, "It's a start. Next time you come, you won't be on those crutches, and will feel more comfortable."

He could read her fairly well, but he did not realize it was the size and power of the horses that made her nervous, not the awkward crutches.

"Now, Love My Gemini ,over there," he pointed. "Is four. She's racing this year, and it's her second year, so we expect she'll do well. Last year she was still learning. Gemini was sired by Capella, and her dam was Gemini."

"They take on the names of the parents?"

"Sometimes, yes. Especially if they have good bloodlines. Capella is still racing. But Gemini is happier being a mother, I think."

Phyllis had joined them in the stables, and now she spoke up. "You're happier when she is a mother, that's what it is." She turned to Suki. "Gemini was tripped in a race and fell. He worries about her since then. She would start a race, and then choke. I do think she likes being a mother, but make no mistake," she smiled. "Phillip mothers her."

Maternal instincts in a male, especially a male as

manly as Phillip, were a thing Suki had never encountered. Her eyes widened.

"I care for those I love." He shrugged. "It's how I am."

Capella snorted, and Phillip turned his attention to the stallion, who had his head leaning out over his stall door. "Capella is fifteen hands high, and he is one of the taller ones here."

"Is he the one you ride?"

Phyllis laughed. "Oh no. We don't ride these horses. Their trainers and the jockeys ride them. We have other horses we ride, if we want to go for a ride. Our racehorses, these we pamper and prep for the races, and then if we do everything right, we make money. Or we lose, and then we try again."

"If you wanted to learn to ride," he said, "we would put you on a smaller horse. A less high-spirited horse. I would love to teach you to ride, but that would be many months after your foot was fully healed. I wouldn't want to risk you re-inuring it."

"You see," Phyllis said, "He will mother you now. Let me show you Sweet On Betsy. She's racing this year too. So we have three entered this year." Phyllis led her to another stall, where a beautiful black horse stood.

This horse had a white spot on her nose, and her coat was shiny and sleek.

"She's beautiful," Suki said.

"I think so too," Phyllis said. "She is my favorite."

Enzo had followed them to the stables, and Suki noticed him lurking in the doorway.

Why did he have to follow us to the stables? We're just looking at horses for goodness sake. It isn't as Phillip and I are in a stall necking.

But now that the thought had occurred to her, she liked the idea very much.

Philip in a stall with his shirt off, kissing her…

What a wonderful way to end the afternoon that would be.

But I can't. I'm Frank's girl and that is why Enzo is following me. Because Frank doesn't trust me, and that is a big problem.

"All your horses are beautiful," Suki said to the siblings. "Thank you for showing them to me."

"Any time," Phyllis said.

"My pleasure," Phillip said.

"I wonder if we might have a bit more of that fruity drink," Suki said. "It was delicious. You must tell me how to make it. I've never seen oranges floating in a drink. I was tempted to eat my slice."

"Sangria is made with wine and fruit," Phyllis said. "I can give you many recipes that are variations. And you absolutely can eat the fruit. It soaks up the alcohol!" She laughed, and Suki started laughing too.

"Well then, I really must eat the fruit," Suki said. "Wouldn't want to waste a drop."

"Let's go back inside, and I'll have Esmeralda

pour another batch for us," Phyllis said. "And then I will tell you all about learning to ride horses, when we were children growing up in Spain."

Today is the day.

Once this blasted cast is off, I'll swim, and wiggle my toes, and dance, and do everything I couldn't do before.

Every. Little. Thing.

Suki could hardly wait. Phyllis was picking her up, and driving her to the doctor's office.

Phyllis was the first female friend Suki had, who had her own car to drive.

In Chicago all the gals she knew either walked, or bummed a ride, or took the bus, or a taxi where they needed to go.

This would be the best girl's day out ever. First the doctor's appointment, then lunch, and then shoe shopping.

Phyllis insisted the big event deserved a new pair of shoes for Suki, and though that hadn't occurred to her, Suki's mind being completely on the doctor visit, she quite agreed with her new best friend.

What they hadn't counted on, was that an unhappy Enzo would follow Suki.

His black car and his glowering expression hovered behind them, like a dark rain cloud.

Suki wondered if Frank would explode on the

phone again, when he called, or if he'd be even a little bit understanding.

When they reached the doctor's office, Enzo insisted on following them inside.

As she filled out the paperwork the doctor needed, she shook her head once.

What a strange trio we make. Two flappers, one in silk pajamas and a cast, one a Spanish socialite, and one hulking man in a dark suit.

Phyllis leaned in, so Enzo couldn't hear. "For goodness' sake, the man hovers like a gorilla," she said.

"I know," Suki said in a low voice, "But it's hard to get upset with him, when he's only doing his job, and doing what Frank tells him to."

She handed the papers to the receptionist, and then went over to Enzo. "You don't need to go back there with me. The doctor is just going to cut my cast off."

"Frank says otherwise. I'm going to watch, make sure nothing happens."

"Oh for goodness sake," Suki said, frustration filling her.

Frank was the one she was upset with.

It really isn't Enzo's fault. But this is ridiculous.

Can't he sit in the waiting room this one time?

Finally they called her back, and she hobbled down the hall, followed by Phyllis, and then Enzo.

She went into the room the nurse indicated, and sat on the examining table.

Phyllis sat in the one chair, and Enzo leaned up against the wall, his arms crossed, which made him look meaner. He appeared the sort of guy who would break somebody's face.

Shortly afterward the doctor came in and, seeing the three of them, pulled his head back in surprise. "Well, hello! I understand you want this cast off, young lady."

"Yes I do. It's been six weeks, and it's time." Suki nodded.

She'd never been more ready for a doctor visit in her life.

"Please cut this thing off of me."

"I understand you were treated by a doctor in Chicago, before you traveled here."

"Yes, that's right." She nodded. "I was told to come here, to have it removed today. I'm ready."

"Let's see what we have here." The doctor examined the cast, where the plaster had begun to crumble. "What have you been doing?"

He looked up at her, and gave her a stern look. "I hope you haven't been on your feet too much."

"Well, I did need to travel here."

He shook his head. "You've been on it more than just to travel here. Look at the way it's begun to crumble. I hope your foot has healed, and you haven't overdone it. Didn't your Chicago doctor tell you to stay off of your foot?"

"Well, yes." She glanced at Enzo, who had an even greater scowl on his brow.

Oh no. I can just imagine what he'll be telling Frank.

The doctor took out a saw, and began to cut through the cast.

Enzo's scowl went deeper, as he watched the doctor use the saw.

Suki hoped Enzo didn't make the doctor so nervous that he messed up with that saw.

It was as if Enzo waited for a reason to jump on the doctor.

Once the doctor cut through the outer layers, he put the saw away, and reached for his scissors.

Enzo's scowl lessened, and Suki relaxed.

The doctor glanced at them both. "You didn't think I was going to use the saw to cut all the way through to your skin?"

"Well, yes," Suki said. "And I'm real glad you didn't."

The doctor cut the rest of the cast away with the scissors, and then pulled it away from her leg and foot, before chucking it into the trash can where it made a loud thud.

Suki looked down at the dry, scaly skin that had been covered by the cast. "Eww."

"Those are just dead skin cells that had nowhere to go," the doctor said. "It's common."

The nurse came in then, and got out alcohol and a cloth. She began to clean Suki's leg and foot.

"Oh that feels wonderful." Suki sighed, and wiggled her toes. "I never want to wear a boot or a shoe again."

"Then I guess we don't need to go shoe shopping," Phyllis said.

"I do need a new pair of dance shoes," Suki said. "Still, wouldn't it be lovely if we never had to wear shoes?"

"I like my heels," Phyllis said. "They display the leg so nicely."

"Now," the doctor said, "Let's see that foot."

Suki noticed he waited until after her foot was cleaned off, to examine it.

After poking and prodding he said, "I believe you are healed enough to walk on it now, and I don't foresee any problems, but if you have a problem with it, come back, and I'll examine your foot again."

"No x-ray?" Enzo said, his voice surprising Suki.

"No, she'd have to go to the hospital for that," the doctor said.

"Or the shoe store," Suki said with a laugh.

None of the others got the joke. Only Frank would have.

"Well, let's go buy you some new shoes," Phyllis said.

"Sounds good to me," Suki took the shoe she had

carried in, which matched the one she had worn in, and slipped it onto her foot.

As she stood, it felt strange to be out of the cast again.

But it also felt good.

THE NEXT MORNING she stood at the edge of the pool, ready to get into the water which had tempted her since her first day at the hotel. Tempted her with how good it would feel to float, and kick, and move in the water.

At last Suki was able to swim, now that the blasted cast was off.

It felt wonderful to move slowly down the steps, and into the warm water. With a push, she was off, swimming, kicking her legs and feet.

Her right foot felt stiff and sore, and like it didn't belong to her, but still she kicked and swam, hoping it would soon be easier, and feel better.

Phyllis dove in, and then swam one length of the pool and back again, before swimming up to Suki.

They did laps together, and after about thirty minutes of swimming, she swam over to Suki.

"Now that your foot is better, I must teach you all the dances," she said.

"Yes! I can't wait! Let's go do it now," Suki said. "Come back to my room."

"Do you have music?"

Suki's expression of joy fell. "No."

"Never you mind that. I'll have that fixed in a jiffy," Phyllis said.

True to her word, she did just that. Calling down to the front desk, Phyllis made arrangements for them to send up a phonograph.

By the time they had changed out of their wet bathing suits, into dry clothes, there was a knock on the door.

Two men were there to deliver the equipment and set it up.

Soon, music was playing, and Phyllis began teaching Suki all the latest dances, the Black Bottom, and the Charleston.

Suki, being a dancer, picked them up right away, with ease and gracefulness.

It felt wonderful to be dancing again. Dance was freedom.

FRANK WAS BACK. The first thing he'd done was come straight to Suki's room to give her a talking to.

That had been hours ago.

He'd spanked her really hard, and then made passionate love to her. She was thoroughly worn out by the time they ate a later dinner on her balcony.

They'd finished dinner, and now they were in

her room waiting for room service to remove their trays, so they would be alone.

She stepped through the door onto the balcony, into the cool night air. The moment she did, he turned, and their eyes met.

Hers uncertain.

His cool and remote.

When she moistened her lips his stare shifted, changed to a look of burning intensity.

Without hesitation, he strode toward her, pulled her into his arms, and his mouth crushed hers. His kiss was full of heat, power, and determination.

She swayed on her feet, as need washed through her. Her lips parted under his relentless assault, welcomed the invasion of his tongue, and her arms slid up around his neck.

He moved her back up against the wall, as their kiss grew wetter, hotter, and hungrier.

Their passion hadn't faded. It had only grown stronger from time apart. They couldn't keep their hands off of each other.

They were outside on the balcony, where anyone might see, as light from the room spilled out to where they stood, but she didn't care.

Let them see.

"I want you," he growled against the side of her neck, his teeth grazing her skin.

Goose bumps rose wherever he touched.

"You're mine," he growled again. "I need you."

Her breathing hitched, as his hands moved up beneath her pajama top, and then unbuttoned it in a hurry, until it and her breasts hung free.

He pulled it off her shoulders, and she let it fall to the concrete.

She wanted him. Now. She understood his need.

He understood hers.

She moaned as his hands slid into her hair, holding her in place, as he ravished her mouth. Her need grew.

He kissed her deep, taking control of her body. He pinned her against the wall, making it clear, he was in charge.

She gasped as he bent his head and kissed her, setting his mouth firmly over hers, testing the full- ness of her lips under his.

For a moment she placed her hands on his chest, and then her lips softened and parted, and she kissed him back, her body melting against his.

The kissing alone was enough to make her stop thinking, as she let him take her to a place of passion.

It had been like this from their first time. His passion always swept her away.

She only thought of ending things between them, when they were apart. Together there was so much passion, she couldn't think. She could only be. With Frank. She was very much his moll.

But they never spoke of love.

~

SUKI WAS EXCITED to be going to the horse races for the first time.

Frank was taking her to meet Al Capone, his men, and their dames. They would all sit together in the section of the club reserved for Al and his guests.

She leaned forward, to look out the window, as they turned onto the grounds of The Miami Jockey Club.

The large sprawling property had been landscaped with beautiful pink flowers, trees, and a white fountain.

"Oh Frank, it's beautiful," she said, clasping her hands together. "Thank you for bringing me here."

"You're welcome," he said. "Remember to thank Mr. Capone."

"Oh, of course," she said.

She'd never sat with Mr. Capone all evening before, and she'd do her best to be a credit to Frank. She was wearing the new dress, hat and shoes that Phyllis had helped her pick out.

The outfit was more elegant than anything else she owned, and the blue matched her eyes. Suki knew she looked good.

The men and women would wear more conservative clothes to this event, not flapper dresses, Phyllis had told her.

"Phyllis took me shopping, and showed me what

the ladies would be wearing," she said. "She's been wonderful. And I can't wait for you to meet her. And her twin brother."

Frank just grunted.

"Do you like my new dress?"

"Yeah. You look good," he said. "That's a nice color on you." He reached into his pocket, and pulled out a box, placing it on the seat between them. "Got you something."

"Oh Frank," she said. "You're so good to me."

"Glad you remembered that," he said. "Open it up."

She picked up the box, and opened it. Inside was a pearl bracelet that had three rows of pearls.

"Frank," she exclaimed. "It's stunning!"

"Put it on."

She put it around her wrist, and turned her wrist this way and that, as she admired it.

"I love it, Frank." She scooted over next to him on the car's seat.

He wrapped one arm around her. "I don't mind you shopping with a girlfriend, or lounging by the pool, and playing games. I don't mind if you go shopping with her, or go to see her house, and her horses. But you just remember when you are out, you are my gal, and you remember rule number one."

"Of course Frank." She nodded. "There are no other men."

He gave her a look, and raised an eyebrow.

Why did he doubt her? She hadn't done anything wrong.

"It's not my fault she has a twin," she said. "Did you know twins sometimes know what the other is thinking? They do a lot of things together, but it's because they're twins. He's always a gentleman. You'll see when you meet him. And he's often away on business. She likes to see him, when he's home. That's all."

Was she explaining too much? Making it worse?

They'd pulled into the parking lot and stopped. He hadn't said another word. Just listened to her ramble.

She touched his thigh, and changed the subject quick. "I wish we could find a private room here somewhere, so I can thank you properly for this gift."

"You can thank me tonight," he said. "Wear nothing but that bracelet when you thank me."

"Oh Frank," she said. "You know how hot that kind of talk makes me."

He opened the door. "We don't want to be late."

"Oh, of course not." She couldn't gage his mood, but knew not to mention the twins any more.

The twins each had a horse in the races today, but she wouldn't say any more about them. She did plan on betting on each of their horses.

They walked to the stands, and climbed the steps up to where Al had a section reserved, under the roof. High enough to be under the shade, and low enough to be closer to the racetrack.

His section was full of men in dark suits, and women all dolled up. Everyone had a race form, and seemed in good spirits.

Of course no one had lost any money yet. Hopefully none of them were poor losers.

They went up to Al first. "Mr. Capone, this is Miss Suki Chesterfield," Frank said.

"Nice to meet you, Suki," Al said, his tone genial. "I saw you at the Green Mill, the night you were injured. Glad you're well enough to join us tonight."

"It's a pleasure to meet you, Mr. Capone," she said. "I remember seeing you too, and I'm glad you weren't hurt. Thank you for inviting me."

"It's nothing," Mr. Capone shrugged. "Frank's dame is always welcome. I've seen you dance at the Green Mill. But now you're Frank's girl. So no more dancing there. You can call me Al. You're family now. You need anything, and can't reach Frank, you come to me."

Suki smiled at him. "Thank you, Al."

Al gave her a kiss on the cheek that felt like a blessing of some sort.

Everyone had witnessed it.

Family. I'm really in with them, now. Whether I want to be or not.

Next Frank introduced her to everyone, and then they all sat down in their seats. Frank pulled her

193

onto his lap, which he frequently did in public. He had to always be touching her, showing everyone that she was his.

He took the racing form and began to explain to her how the races worked. "There are ten horses in each race, see?" He pointed to the first race. "Now you can bet to win, to place or to show. On any of these ten. Win is first place, and to place is second, and third is to show. So you pick the horse you think will win. Then you can pick another for second, and another for third. Or you can bet on just one horse."

"I see," she said. "And what about the odds?"

"That's more complicated," he said. "Don't worry about it. You just stick to win, place, and show, and have fun."

He was speaking to her as if she were a twelve-year-old girl who wouldn't understand. It irked her more than a little when he did this, but she didn't want to make a fuss in front of the others. She really just wanted to enjoy herself.

But she couldn't help thinking, *I bet if Phillip were sitting here, next to me he'd explain the odds, and not speak to me as if I were a child. He'd tell me about the horses, and help me pick a winner.*

"They'll come around to Al's section, and then we'll place the bets," Frank was saying. "The runners go back and forth, so we don't have to leave our seats."

She tried not to think of Phillip, but to turn her

full attention to Frank. He'd given her money before they left the hotel, so she had money of her own for betting, but she'd seen the large roll of cash he had.

He would either be losing big, or winning big, if he bet all that money. But losing a big stash would not faze him at all.

Having to scramble for money, even after she got work as a dancer, she didn't know if she was capable of betting big. To be that free with money, and to chance losing it all, that might be further than she could go.

He seemed to have the attitude that if he ran out of money, he'd just go make more of it.

She sat looking at all the ladies sun hats, parasols and umbrellas. The multi colored hats brought color and liveliness to the crowd of men, some in dark suit, and some in light colored summer suits. Everyone was dressed fine enough for church, or Easter Sunday dinner.

Al's men appeared respectable, and their women did too. You'd never know what they did for their money, if you didn't already know.

The names. They were so much fun.

Taking her pen she looked first for Phillip's horse, and then for Phyllis's horse.

"They'll be bringing the horses out, to walk them around, and let us look at them, down there, in that gated area behind the stands," Frank said. "Do you want to go down and see them, or do you want to stay here, in your seat?"

He was actually asking her. How unusual.

Frank usually told her what to do.

She said, "Yes, I'd like to go see them."

They made their way down the steps again, and over to the area where the horses would come out.

Many in the crowd had come over to view the horses. Al decided to join them, and was enjoying a Cuban cigar as he waited for the horses. The ladies stood either on the concrete, or the grass, while the horses were lead on the dirt path track. The same kind of dirt that was on the track they'd be racing on.

They brought them out, one by one, with their numbers and colors on, and walked them past the spectators.

"They're so tall," Suki said. "When I went to see Phyllis, their horses were tall too."

"Racehorses tend to be tall," Frank said. "And fast. Look at those beauties."

Suki knew she was supposed to be judging which horse would win, but they all looked to her as if they could've, and she had no idea how to judge any of them, other than this one looked prettier to her than the others, and she liked the sound of that one's name.

"They sure are pretty," she said.

"We need to go back to our seats," he said. "And place our bets."

Back in their seats, she randomly picked a horse. "I'd like Call Me Frisky to win."

Frank laughed. "You just like the name," he said.

That was true, but seeing the horses had only made her more confused. Maybe once she'd watched a few races, she'd know more about how to choose a good horse.

By the third race, Suki still hadn't won a thing. But she was still having fun. Just watching the horses race was fun, and she got caught up in the excitement of it.

In the next race, Love my Gemini was racing. Knowing that was Phillip's horse, Suki placed a bet on her. Just two more races away, Capella, his stallion would be racing. In the very last race, Phyllis's horse, Sweet on Betsy would run.

Suki hoped all their horses won.

When Suki bet on Phillip's horse, Frank said nothing, but his eyes narrowed. That told her Frank didn't like Phillip already.

They hadn't even met. Likely he was jealous.

But she'd done nothing wrong. She and Phillip hadn't so much as kissed. They were just friends. It made her happy to spend time with Phillip, but it was best she not let on about that around Frank.

Al and Frank were winning and in good spirits. Hootch was flowing from the flasks in nearly every man's coat pocket.

Suki took another sip of her spiced rum.

She'd lost every race so far but the next race was the one Phillip's horse was in, and she really hoped his horse would win.

He did and she won. Watching Phillip with his winning horse was a thrill, but she tried not to let on too much, or to appear as if she was watching Phillip, instead of his horse. She could genuinely show how excited she was to have won her bet.

She collected her winnings. But then she lost them again, when she bet on Phyllis's horse.

When the races were over, they all said goodbye, and went to get into their cars to go.

As they were driving down the road, Frank said. "We're going home in two days. I'm gonna put you on the train again."

"So soon? But you just got here. We could stay longer," Suki said. "It's beautiful here, and the weather is perfect. Chicago is so cold this time of year."

"Yeah, well, when Al says go, we go."

"Could you stay behind an extra day or two, and then go?"

"Sorry babe," Frank said. "I gotta do my job. We'll come back."

Both were silent on the way back to the hotel.

Suki played with the pearl bracelet, turning and looking at each pearl. She couldn't gauge his mood, so she was silent.

Back in the room, Frank said, "Get naked. Now.

We're meeting everyone for dinner in an hour. I want you naked before we go. You can start thanking me for that bracelet."

She barely had time to get ready, after she was done thanking him to his satisfaction. Her cheeks and chest were flushed, and the flapper dress she was changing into made that blush even more noticeable. She thought about covering with a wrap, though it was warm out.

"Leave that," he said, when he saw her reach for it. "You look like you spent the last hour on your back. I like that."

So, he wants everyone to know we just finished making nookie. Wonder what that's about. Showing me off to everyone. A look what I've got kind of deal.

When she reached for a comb, he took it from her hand, and said, "We're leaving. Now."

As they walked into the restaurant, she knew she looked disheveled.

He bent to whisper in her ear. "We're going to do it again, once for every pearl on that bracelet, before you're allowed to go to sleep."

Her cheeks flamed and her entire body heated.

After they sat at the table, and placed their order, she had he urge to count the pearls on her bracelet.

Three rows of pearls. How many in each row?

Using her fingers, she started counting them, as she twisted the bracelet around.

His hand closed over hers, where her fingers

were counting. "Stop fidgeting. Don't you like the bracelet I bought you?"

"Yes, I love it."

"Then stop fiddling with it."

She stopped, and reached for her water glass, suddenly thirsty as her nerves had made her mouth dry.

He adjusted his napkin on his lap, and then she felt his hand on her knee moving up.

What is he playing at now?

"Two more days, and then we're back home," he said. "Is there anything you want to do, or see, before we go?"

"The elephant. I wasn't able to ride with a cast on. That, and I want to dance. There's a club, and Phyllis said she'd teach me the latest dances."

"We can ride the elephant in the morning, if you don't sleep in," he said with a smirk. "And go to the club tomorrow night."

The rest of the evening they talked with the others, while he played with her leg, off and on drawing circles, reminding her of what awaited later.

Everyone was talking about going back. Now that they'd been to the races, which apparently was the only reason they'd all come to Miami. If they had other reasons, they did not talk about them.

She didn't want to leave Florida, but what choice did she have? Frank was paying the bills, and Mr.

Capone was calling the shots, which meant even Frank wasn't free to do as he pleased.

I need to get my old job back, after we get home. Then I'll save up for another visit. If I pay for it myself, I'll say when I stay, and when I go home. I want to come back to visit Phyllis and Phillip.

Keeping her thoughts to herself made her quieter this evening, but with Frank doing the talking, he did not seem to notice.

After dinner, when they were back in the hotel room, Frank thoroughly wore her out. Every time they stopped to rest, and she'd doze off, he'd wake her again, and count how many times they'd done it, and then add to that number.

When she said, "I'm tired Frank," he said, "I'm going to make this trip is as memorable to you, as it is to me. You'll be too tired to do anything but rest on that train. I'm only here with you for two more days. Now about saying thank you for those pearls..."

By the time the sun rose, she'd had one hour of sleep. She was too tired to even think of riding an elephant. She didn't want to ride anything, and when he asked her about it, she said, "No, I just want to sleep."

He'd smiled real deep, which made her think he might have worn her out on purpose. He'd had her all to himself and she'd had no time for Phylis.

Hungry, he now left her alone and ordered room service.

She didn't know where he got his stamina. Or what he was trying to prove.

Suki didn't see Phyllis or Phillip again. There was no time and she was too tired anyway. Maybe that had been his plan. To keep her from seeing them. She wondered if he knew that she had their phone number. She made a point not to mention them.

They ate, they slept, and they made nookie. It was no different than Chicago. She didn't go out with friends; she didn't see friends, and they didn't come to visit her. It was like being caged again, just that looking out the windows she saw sunshine and palm trees instead of snow.

But it was a cage, just the same. And this time she knew it for what it was. Even the fanciest hotel could be a cage.

The train home was the same train, but it didn't feel the same at all.

She was exhausted from nookie, and not enough sleep. The excitement of going to a new place was gone. The excitement of the train itself was gone too. Phillip wasn't there to keep her company, and keep her spirits up, and there was no one else on the train that she wanted to talk to. Leaving Miami had filled her with sadness.

The loss of time with her friends hit her harder than she had expected. She'd never had friends like Phylis and Phillip before.

Too often friends had let her down, or they had

parted ways and gotten on with their lives, but it had never felt like she was losing something. It had never made her heart heart.

She reached for the spiced rum again, though she didn't need it for her foot. This was a different kind of hurt that she was trying to numb. She stayed in her compartment and mostly slept.

The rocking of the train was the only truly comforting thing as she'd lost her appetite. She missed her friends, and it was easier to sleep than to think about them.

Resigned to picking up her old life in Chicago, she vowed to get her old job back, and to save up for her next visit to Miami to see them again.

Phyllis had given her their phone number, and she had their address. Both were safe in Suki's little beaded bag, so they wouldn't lose touch. She would call Phyllis, when she was home again, and wasn't having to give Frank all her attention.

She missed Florida, and her friends, more than she could ever let on. It was best not to think of them when Frank was in the room. But she thought of them often.

Maybe she would make the next visit to Miami a permanent one.

CHAPTER 8

August 1926
One year and five months later

Suki lay in bed, in her hotel room, at the Arlington Hotel in Hot Springs, Arkansas with ice on her foot, watching the ceiling fan go around and round, as her thoughts went around and around. The rum she'd been sipping all day had gone to her head, and it was like being on a merry-go-round, as the room moved, and her thoughts circled.

Thinkin' about things, just thinkin' about things, like dancing and injuries, and resting, and being on the go so, so much, and not resting enough 'cause I don't take time to rest like I should, and this is a wonderful room in the The Arlington. It's a grand hotel, very fancy. I'm in a great big bed with a ceiling fan over my head, and out my window I can see trees.

Her window faced the street and she could look straight down, and see all the things happening at night. See the nightlife, and all the people out for the evening. Her room was quiet, because it was away from the elevators.

The room was far too quiet to suit Suki, who wanted to be out dancing, and having fun, but she had reinjured her foot dancing the other night and now she couldn't.

Frank had told her not to leave her room.

It reminded her too much of when she had broken her foot, and she was now feeling sorry for herself ,and wondering how she had made such a mess of her life.

She had never made it back to Miami to see her friends and she felt lonelier than she ever had in her life.

The phone on the bedside table rang, and Suki rolled over to reach for it. "Hello."

"How's the Arlington, doll?" Phyllis' musical tone came through the line, and Suki rolled onto her back with a smile.

Phyllis. She called me, all the way from Miami. How nice.

Phyllis had become her best friend. She missed her now. Things always seemed better after talking to Phyllis.

"Are you all settled in?"

"Hello, Phyllis, my dear. So good of you to call. Yes, I am in, so very in. I'm as in, as in can be, here in this room," she giggled. "Surely am in."

"Darling, you are spifflecated," Phyllis said.

"Splendid. That is what I am," Suki said. "Splendid."

"Won't this be fun? Do go on, and tell me everything. Is it your foot? Have you been drinking to cut the pain, again? Should I worry?"

"Oh, I'm a bit wobbly, but nothing to worry about."

"That's good. So, what's bothering you, doll?"

"Not dancing. Not up on a stage any more. Maybe never again. Frank blocks every attempt I make to get a dance gig. Says he doesn't want me dancing on stage any more. He's put the screws to that. No one in town will hire me."

"Well, you're not in Chicago now," Phyllis said. "You don't have to go back there, unless you want to. Tell me about the Arlington. How is your room?"

"My room's hard to describe. It's kind of different."

"How so?"

"It's not a square shape; it's got one straight wall that the bed's on but then it faces out and then there's all these little things like an octagonal kind of a look. It's got a little tiny bathroom with white and black tiles, and a shower, a toilet, and a pedestal sink. And it's not very big. If you were a big person, you wouldn't fit in here very well, but I'm not a big person, so I don't mind it so much. The walls are painted a peachy beige color, and all the trim is off-white. And you're not a big person either, so you'd fit. Oh, do come here and stay. I need some female company, and I miss you."

Suki stopped rambling on, and took a sip of her drink.

"The hotel sounds very nice. And I miss you, too. I've heard it's a grand hotel. Tell me more."

"Oh, it is, I like it," Suki said. "I could stay here, and rest a good long time, because I'm tired; I'm so tired, so very tired I could just close my eyes right now. If I could just get rid of this tension headache in the back of my neck and shoulders, if I could just make that go away, and the ice would make my foot quit throbbing. And if I could just sleep, and sleep, and sleep, until everything felt better, and all my troubles went away, that would be so nice. If I could just stay here for a time, for a good long time. For a good, good, long time."

Taking another sip of her drink, the ice in the glass tinkled against the glass.

"Darling, are you by yourself? Where's Frank? You sound so very down," Phyllis said, concern in her tone.

"I am. By myself. Yes, ma'am," Suki said.

She nodded, even though Phyllis couldn't see her.

"He's off with the guys. No dames allowed. And he's mad, cause I hurt my foot again, dancing. I think he hates me dancing. And I hate being stuck in my room with a bum foot, and not being able to dance. Come visit. Room 541 in The Arlington. Five. Four. One. That's where I am, resting my foot, icing my foot, not sure this foot will ever be right again. 'Cause I broke it once. But I love to dance. I love to dance. Maybe I danced on it more than I should have, after I broke it, because it never quite seems to have healed right. Maybe I don't stay still long enough for it to heal. All I know is, I just want to be better. I want to heal, and be better. I want a healthier life. I want a safe, and healthy life."

Suki sniffed and reached for her glass again.

"Darling, I want that for you, too," Phyllis said.

"I want a safe, and healthy life, somewhere out there. That's all I ever wanted, was to stay safe, healthy, and be able to pay for things myself."

"If you'd stayed in Miami, we'd have found you a job. Or if you'd come here, instead of Hot Springs."

"I had to come here for the baths. Frank insisted," Suki said.

"He's very demanding of you, insisting things all the time."

"He just wants me to get better."

"Well, you know you can always come back to

Miami, and stay with me, if you're tired of always pleasing Frank. Come stay with me, till you get back on your feet, and figure out what you want to do. Is life with Frank in Chicago what you really want? To be his moll, with your life centered on pleasing him? You seemed so much happier in Miami, before he arrived, even with your foot in a cast. Have you ever thought about that? What do *you* want, Suki?"

Suki's gaze went to the ceiling fans again, and her thoughts went into a spin.

I'm tired of pleasing somebody else. I'm tired of pleasing other people. When will it be time for me to just be able to do what I want to do?

"No," she said. "I don't know what I want to do. Frank has been real good to me."

Phyllis was quiet.

The ceiling fan went around, and around, and Suki's thoughts circled again as she watched it.

For the most part I do what I want to do. For the most part I do what I want to do, and yet I always have to please him.

Is that what I really want to do?

Pleasing him is part of the deal, part of that unspoken deal. I please him, and he takes care of me. And that's how it's always been. I please him, and he takes care of me.

But I have to do what he wants me to, and I am so very tired of that. So very tired of everything.

"Back then, you said you wanted to be your old

independent self again. And you've said it more than once, since then. So many times, I've lost count."

Suki didn't answer, as her thoughts moved around, while she watched that ceiling fan.

Independent. Independent. Hmm. I always thought I was. Everybody says I am. Independent. Sassy. Independent and sassy but truth is, maybe I am, or maybe I am not.

Suki sighed. "Maybe I'm not as independent as I thought."

The ceiling fan cast shadows as it moved.

Suki's thoughts wouldn't stop spinning.

Truth is, I'm tired of pleasing him. But he takes care of me. Not sure what I'd do, if I weren't pleasing him, then he wouldn't take care of me. What would I do then?

What would I do without Frank? What would I do without him?

She spoke the words out loud. "I don't know what I'd do without him."

"Aww, Suki, you're all balled up, and you're on a toot right now. You're repeating yourself. It's not a good night for thinking, when you're zozzled."

Suki turned her gaze away from the fan to the window.

That ceiling fan goes 'round and 'round and is making me think all these thoughts in my head. This is the problem with staying still this long. Any time I stay still this long, I have to start thinkin' things.

It's why I hardly ever stay still. I'm always moving, and dancing, and moving, and dancing.

When I stay still I think too much, I think too much when I stay still.

And then everything gets all muddled in my head. With what I did, what I'm doin', what I'm going to do. It gets all muddled in my head. It's just easier to go with a moment by moment, and a now, and stay in this moment, and in this now right now.

I will do this thing, and in the next moment I might, or I might not, do that thing. And that's how I live my life.

She repeated again. "I don't know what I'd do without him."

Phyllis had gone silent.

"You still there?" Suki asked.

"Yes, doll. I'm here, listening."

"My feet aren't right, that's the problem. My feet will never be right. I'll never dance again. Everything I had is gone."

"It's just one foot, Suki. And your foot is just sprained, not broken, remember? I was there when the doctor took the cast off, and he checked your foot, and said the bone was healed. You're just confused right now. It's the rum. We can talk about this again later. Try not to think of all these unhappy things, and get some rest. You'll feel better in the morning."

"Okay," Suki said.

"Goodnight, Suki. Now try to sleep."

"Goodnight, Phyllis." She hung up the phone, and took the now-melted ice and towel off her foot, and then took it into the bathroom to toss it into the bathtub.

Catching a glimpse of herself, she leaned in toward the mirror. Reddened, sad eyes stared back at her.

Pulling back, she shook her head.

This is no good, all this thinking. Phyllis is right. Tonight's not the night. Tomorrow I'll think about it.

She didn't bother taking her makeup off, but she did change into her silk pajamas. She came out of the bathroom, picked up her silver flask, and went to pour herself a fresh drink. The flask was empty.

Her gaze swept the room, taking in the clothes and shoes cluttering up the room.

Nearly every item of clothing in this room, Frank had bought for her. The silver flask with the "S" on it was now empty. Frank had bought that flask for her, and usually kept her flush with rum, so that it was almost never empty. He never let her run out of rum.

Tonight the rum was gone.

It was the last thought she had before falling asleep.

~

A FEW DAYS LATER, when Suki could be up on her feet again, she went down to the shops on the bottom level of the hotel.

Suki noted the young blonde with bobbed hair and the long dress looking at a beautiful beaded flapper dress in the shop.

"That one would look good on you," Suki said.

The cute blonde turned to meet Suki's gaze.

"I don't have the money for that dress or any other," the girl replied. "I spent all my money on my new haircut. The first haircut I've ever had."

Suki eyed the new haircut, which didn't go with the girl's old-fashioned dress.

"So that's why you're wearing such a dowdy old dress." Suki swept her gaze over the girl, from head to toe, and back up again. "You've started a metamorphosis you can't finish."

The girl looked so dejected, and suddenly Suki knew just what to do.

I have plenty of dresses, she thought. *I can help her metamorphosis along, so the young butterfly can fly away and be independent.*

"Don't be so sad, doll face." Suki laughed. "I can fix you up. Your hair looks good. You could be a stunner. You just need a little help. I'm Suki." She stuck out her hand.

The girl smiled, reached out, and shook it. "I'm Bethany."

"Whoa, that's an old-fashioned name. We'll work

on that. Come on up to my room," Suki said. "I'll get you fixed up in a jiff. A dress, some makeup, the works. We'll put on our glad rags, and you'll be ready to hit the town."

She gestured to her to follow and headed for the elevator.

"Oh gosh, Suki, that'll be wonderful. Thank you."

Suki laughed again. "Any time. I've got more clothes than I need. I only have to ask for what I want, 'cause my sugar daddy's real good to me."

The elevator opened, and they stepped inside. Suki pushed the button for the fourth four.

Bethany looked nervous. "You're on four?"

What had her so nervous? Surely, she's not afraid to go to my room.

"Why, yes. I am. That's why I pressed it."

Where did she think we were going, the roof?

Bethany stood frowning at the number four on the elevator panel.

Why does so look so worried?

"Don't worry, doll, I have just the thing," Suki said. "You'll be all dolled up in no time." Impatient, Suki tapped the toe of her shoe on the elevator floor. "These elevators are so slow."

When the door finally opened, she rushed out and reached into her purse for her key.

Bethany followed along behind her.

When she unlocked the door to her room Bethany followed her in, closed the door behind her, and gasped in amazement at the sight of dresses and hats flung everywhere. Boas, feathers, and shoes were scattered about, and empty bottles of champagne sat on every surface.

Suki grasped Bethany by the hand, pulled her over to a wardrobe, and flung it open. Dresses in many colors hung inside.

"Oh, they're all so pretty," Bethany said.

Suki just smiled.

"First, though," Suki said, still holding Bethany's hand and swinging it as if they were schoolgirls. "Your old things have to go."

Bethany appeared to be close to giggling.

This is going to be fun.

Suki helped Bethany out of her dress and then her slip. Her corset, hose, and panties remained.

"Turn around," Suki said.

Bethany turned and faced the full-length mirror.

Suki took the scissors and began to cut the corset strings.

Snip. Snip. Snip.

The back of Bethany's corset pulled apart on each side, and the cold steel of the scissors met her back. She shivered, and goose bumps broke out across her skin. When the corset dropped, she caught it and held it, her cheeks heating as her breasts bobbed.

Clearly, she was embarrassed.

Unaffected by Bethany's semi-nudity, Suki

whisked the corset out of her hands and away. "We can burn this thing, if you like," she said. "Some women do."

"Oh, no. I wouldn't want to start a fire." Bethany cupped her breasts in modesty.

Oh, for goodness' sake, Suki thought. *We're both women. Why is she so shy about her breasts? It's not as if we both haven't seen bare breasts before. There are no men around. It's just us. No reason to be jumpy.*

How young and innocent she is. Was I ever like that?

"Always the good girl, aren't you?" Suki grinned.

"Well, I—" Bethany frowned and looked down at her feet. "I guess."

Suki tossed the corset into the metal trashcan behind Bethany and the thud startled the girl. She jumped but she didn't look up.

She's as jumpy as that new colt Phillip showed me.

"Take a deep breath," Suki said. "You're free now."

Bethany took a breath and then let it out, but her breath was shallow and not the relaxed kind.

"That wasn't deep." Suki placed her hands on Bethany's waist. "Your waist is so small. Almost too small, from wearing those corsets. Whoever invented them should be shot. A woman can't breathe in one of those things. She can't move much, and she sure as hell isn't free. Doesn't this feel better already?" She moved her hands up to touch the bottom of Bethany's ribs. "You can expand more here, take a breath, and really breathe."

"Yes, I guess." Bethany's voice came out unsure.

"Seriously." Suki stilled her hands. "Take a deep breath. I mean it. I want to show you something."

Bethany took another short, up-high, breath.

"Not like that. That's a little breath. I want you to fill your lungs all the way down to here." Suki touched Bethany's rib cage where she wanted Bethany to breathe in deep. "Push your ribcage out to the side as it expands when you breathe in. Push against my hands."

Bethany took a deep breath.

"More."

Bethany breathed deeper, and the bottom of her rib cage moved out a little more.

"That's it. Feel how your ribs press against my hands. Take more deep breaths like that."

After Bethany practiced a few more minutes of deep breathing, Suki released her. "Now you've got it. Let go and keep breathing deep. It's good for you. Make you feel like a new woman."

A slow smile spread across Bethany's face.

Finally, the girl understood.

Suki smiled back at her.

"Better?" Suki perched on the arm of a chair and reached for a cigarette.

"Yes. Much better."

"Good." Placing the cigarette in a long silver

holder, Suki reached for a lighter and flicked it. She lit the cigarette and then inhaled. "Ciggy?"

"No, thank you. I don't smoke."

Silence hovered for a moment.

Finally, to break the silence, Suki asked, "Are you embarrassed by your breasts?"

"Oh. Well, no. I guess not." Bethany dropped her hands to her sides. "It's just that, no one but my aunt and my doctor have ever seen them. I'm not used to anyone else looking at them."

Well, that explains a lot. She's an innocent. Probably never even kissed a man.

"They're quite big for someone with your small frame," Suki said.

"Yes, my aunt took me to the doctor about it when I was younger. She even asked the doctor about them, but he said they were perfectly normal and they just kept growing."

Didn't she know hers were like the ones you'd see in a museum by one of the great sculptors? Perfect in every way. Did she never look at herself in the mirror?

"Oh, they're perfect. Perfect, round, and melon-like." Suki inhaled again, and then blew out a line of smoke. "I've never seen any so peachy perfect."

"Have you seen many?" Bethany's eyes were full of surprise and curiosity. The kind that got innocent young girls into trouble.

This one needed a big sister to look after her.

"Sure, doll. If you go to petting parties, you're bound to see 'em." Suki laughed.

If she only knew how wild those parties can get. She might just see a whole lot more than a few women's breasts at the wilder ones.

Bethany stared at her, a puzzled look on her face.

Suddenly Suki realized her dress wasn't going to fit Bethany unless she bound her, because her curves were too full.

"We'll have to bind you."

"Bind me?" Bethany's voice squeaked.

"Your breasts, doll face. They're not in fashion, so we'll have to bind them. Too much jiggle, you know." Suki laughed. "Give one of your shoulders a shake, and you'll see." Jiggling her shoulders in a shoulder shimmy, she demonstrated the move. "Try it."

Bethany imitated the movement, and her breasts jiggled. Widening her eyes, she reached to cover them again.

Suki laughed so hard her shoulders shook. "Can you imagine how much they'd bounce if you did the Charleston or the shimmy? Honey, when you shimmy, you're still gonna have plenty of shaking going on. Yet if they're bound, you won't put out anyone's eye."

Bethany giggled, and kept giggling.

Oh, it's fun helping Bethany. So much fun.

Suki found a roll of white gauze in the dresser

drawer, and wrapped it around Bethany's breasts, binding them to her chest.

There, she thought. *It won't give her the boyish, flat-chested look, but at least it will partially contain the jiggle, as well as making the dress fit.*

Looking for the dress she had in mind, Suki pulled out a heavily beaded golden dress with gold beading, thin straps, and a drop waist.

"You can have this one. I never wear it anymore, and it's the perfect color with your hair."

She handed Bethany the dress.

"Thank you." Slipping the soft, silky gold dress over her head, Bethany adjusted it around her hips and looked in the mirror.

Suki watched the smile spreading across Bethany's face. The girl in the mirror with the pale skin and blonde hair wearing the gold dress now had a glow about her. The glow of happiness.

Seeing her so happy made Suki happy, too.

Suki adjusted the dress at Bethany's hips. "Your hips are almost too curvy for this dress. We can't do anything about it, though. It'll do." She stepped back. "You need either a cloche hat or a beaded headband to match."

"Yes. All of my hats are too big," Bethany said.

"Too old-fashioned, you mean. That's what happens when you let an old bluenose pick out your clothes."

"True." Bethany agreed.

Suki paused with her hand on her hip, surveying Bethany from head to toe. "Golden from head to toe. That color really does suit you, but now you need a splash of color. Where's your lipstick?"

"I don't have any. I'm not allowed to wear makeup."

Suki raised an eyebrow in surprise. "Really?"

"That's the truth."

Suki knew it was.

The poor child, she was soon to be a woman. She was going to be out in the world not knowing anything about being a woman.

'Not allowed to.' Those words grated on Suki's nerves.

The poor girl isn't allowed to do anything or have any fun. How terrible. Something has to be done.

"Well, I can fix that in a jiffy." She went into the bathroom and rummaged through her case filled with makeup. "Red. Every woman should at least have one tube. Men love it when a woman wears red."

She stepped out of the bathroom and held a lipstick tube out to Bethany. "This is the ticket."

"I don't know." Appearing uncertain, Bethany took the lipstick from her and opened the lid. "It's very red."

"Go on." Suki waved her toward the bathroom mirror. "Try it out."

Bethany went into the bathroom and applied the lipstick to her lips, then stared into the mirror.

"I don't know, Suki. It's very bright."

"Let me see." Suki came up behind her.

The red stood out against Bethany's pale skin, just as it should. "Doll face, it's perfect. You have the perfect little bow-shaped mouth. Men will line up to kiss you."

Bethany blushed and giggled.

"You can keep that one." Suki gestured to the lipstick. "I have others."

"Thank you."

"I can't give you any stockings, because I've ruined all mine, and need to buy some new ones, but you'll need a different kind anyway."

"Suki, you've already done so much."

"Not so much." Suki shrugged. "Now listen, doll. The latest fashion is to roll your stockings down to your knees."

"Oh." Bethany's eyes lit in surprise. "How do they stay up without a garter belt?"

"Sometimes they don't." Suki laughed. "Some of us even roll them down below the knee. You'll see when we go dancing."

"I can't wait to learn all the dances."

"I can teach you. Right now, though," Suki reached into the back of the wardrobe, for her silver flask, "it's time to celebrate your freedom."

"Oh, oh, I don't know." Bethany shook her head, and leaned away from it.

Suki drew her brows together. "Don't be a wet blanket, doll."

In an unsure voice Bethany said, "All right. I'll try it."

"Now you're on the trolley."

Suki handed Bethany the silver flask Frank had given her with the "S" engraved on the front.

Raising the flask to her lips, Bethany took a small sip of the liquid inside. She swallowed, blinked, and coughed.

Suki watched her with amusement. With approval, she noted Bethany took her first taste more like an adult than a child.

She'd be an adult soon enough. Better for her to learn about the world from a safe friend, who was like an older sister, than to learn it on the street, fast.

There were many who would not look after her and who would, instead, take every advantage.

Bethany handed the flask back to Suki. "What is it?"

"Rum. It's imported and can be hard to get, unless you know the right people."

"You must know the right person."

Suki laughed. "Doll face, I know *all* the right people."

Bethany laughed with her, and another smile spread across her face.

"Come to the club with me tonight, and I'll introduce you to them," Suki said. "They'll love you."

"Tonight, I have a date. We're going to see the new Rudolph Valentino movie."

"Oh, yeah. I'm gonna see it on Saturday night. Frank has some business to conduct tonight, so I'm just hanging out at the club," Suki said.

"I wish I could go with you."

"Next time, doll face. You go have fun at the movie." The phone rang.

That had to be Frank, doing his usual check-in to see what she was up to.

Suki answered the phone. "Hello?"

"Suki, you behaving yourself?"

"Oh. Hi, Frank." She winked at Bethany as she purred into the phone. "I miss you already."

Bethany gathered her old clothes, turned back to Suki, and whispered, "Thank you."

Suki waved one hand at her, while holding the phone with the other. She lay back on her bed, listening to Frank, as she watched Bethany slip out the door.

CHAPTER 9

*F*rom across the room Suki watched Rocco guide Bethany into the club, his hand on the small of her back.

So, she's taken up with Rocco. That didn't take long.

But then, Rocco moves fast when he sees what he wants. I'm glad Frank and I got together before Rocco decided he wanted me enough to pursue. Frank put a stop to that right away.

That's one of the pluses of being with Frank. He keeps all the other men away, so none of them bother me anymore.

Music played as flappers and their dates made their way inside. All the women wore summer dresses with dropped waists, intricate beading, and long ropes of pearls.

Inside the club, white tablecloths covered the round tables and crystal candleholders holding lit candles sat in the middle of each one. Everyone had a drink, and the crystal glasses and wine goblets caught the light of the flickering candles. Large chandeliers lit up the dance floor in front of the band.

The musicians played the Charleston as dancers stepped high.

Suki couldn't wait. She'd be dancing all evening, now that her foot was better.

Rocco led Bethany to a table, near the front of the dance floor, marked by a reserved sign.

One of the waiters plucked the sign off the table, and then held out a chair for her.

Suki made her way across the room, over to her. "Bethany, you're here. I see you've met Rocco. That's Frank." She pointed to Frank, who'd walked over to whisper in Al Capone's ear.

Mr. Capone nodded, and Frank went over to the bar to talk to the bartender.

"They've got business to discuss," Suki said. "Do you want some champagne?"

"None for her tonight, Suki," Rocco said. "She was spiffilcated before we even left the track. Can't send my little baby home, in that condition so soon."

"Yours, Rocco?" Suki wondered how invested he was in making Bethany his girl.

"Mine."

That was the answer she was afraid of. "Want her all to yourself, do you?"

"As I said, mine."

"That was fast. Over the Canton twins so soon?"

"Leave it, Suki." He glowered at her, but she wasn't afraid of him.

She was Frank's girl. And no one messed with Frank's girl. So, she could say whatever she wanted to Rocco.

Still, it was best not to poke the bear, as her mother used to tell her.

"Come on, doll face." Suki turned to Bethany, who appeared bewildered by the conversation. "You ready to dance?"

"Oh, yes." Bethany had been tapping her toes. "I can't wait to learn the Charleston."

"Oh, that's not even the newest dance." Suki sipped her champagne, and then set her glass on the table, ready to go. "It's the Black Bottom. Come on. I'll teach you."

Suki taught Bethany all the new dances, and Bethany seemed to be having a good time, while Rocco watched them from his table.

A policeman had entered the bar, and was moving slow, but Suki didn't take much note of it, as everyone knew the police in Hot Springs looked the other way, and the mayor was a gangster, too. It was a dirty town. Everyone was paid off.

As long as no fights broke out, this was the perfect vacation spot for Al and his gang. So, Suki hadn't paid any attention to the lone officer.

But suddenly he was behind Bethany, tapping her on the shoulder.

What could he possibly want with such a sweet young girl? She's the kind of girl who probably asks permission to swipe the fresh cookies your mother just baked.

Bethany turned to see who'd tapped her on the shoulder. Seeing the policeman, she stopped dancing, and froze on the dance floor.

Dancers around them moved away as if she had the plague.

"Miss Robinson, this isn't the place for a woman your age." He gestured at the tables where Al Capone and his men sat.

Al leaned toward Rocco, and spoke to him, as they both watched the policeman.

"Have you been keeping company with those men?" the officer asked Bethany.

Rocco, who'd been half out of his seat, leaned back, restrained by whatever Al had said to him. But he looked ready to spring into violence at any moment.

Suki knew how to defuse a situation when it came to cops. She'd had plenty of practice talking to them, whenever her mother had needed help to get rid of a man who'd begun to treat her bad. Suki never dreaded the cops coming, because they brought an end to the danger and violence, as long as they were there.

"No, daddy, she's with me." Suki interrupted, and threaded her arm through Bethany's, and then winked at him. "She just wants to learn the new dances. See?"

"That's right," Bethany agreed. "Suki promised to teach me the dances."

"So, she's been a good little doll this evening," Suki added. "In a couple of days, she'll be eighteen, and then she can do whatever she wants."

"Be that as it may, she's not eighteen yet. I'm sure Mr. Capone doesn't want to have to deal with this kind of situation while he's on vacation, trying to relax." He nodded at Suki, and then addressed Bethany again. "Your aunt and uncle are worried. They filed a missing person's report. You'll have to come with me."

"Yes, sir." Cheeks blazing, Bethany walked toward the door with the policeman.

Rocco's steady gaze watched her go.

Bethany turned toward Suki, and mouthed, "Thank you."

Suki blew her a kiss and winked, before Bethany went out the door.

Likely there'd be hell to pay with her aunt and uncle. But she'd be of age in a few days, and then they'd have less of a stranglehold over her.

I'll check on her in a couple days, if I haven't heard from her by her birthday.

CHAPTER 10

Suki groaned. It was almost noon. She'd slept in and the sun was pouring through the window, hurting her eyes. They'd been up late last night as usual, dancing, drinking, having a ball. Today she was tired and feeling her age, feeling older than her age. And that had been happening more lately, especially since young Bethany, had walked into her life, reminding her what it was to be young, naïve, and innocent with the whole world stretching out at her fingertips.

She sat up, stretched and reached for a cigarette.

But really, no, really, she'd never been young and naïve like Bethany. She hadn't had the kind of life that had allowed for it. Her life had been rough from the start.

Dancing was a way out, dancing was good times.

Happier people. No more raised fists, well, most of the time.

Hanging with Al and his gang, there was always a slight danger of that, but for the most part, the guys treated the gals pretty darn good.

Her gaze swept the room across dresses draped over chairs, pearls, makeup, silk stockings, and heels.

Yeah, I've lived pretty well. Since Frank stepped in.

Any time I want to buy something I just do. I don't even have to look at the price tags. He'll take care of it.

She was happy to be his moll.

Because he's Mr. Money bags and can buy whatever I want. So, why am I so sad? Aah. All this thinking is no good. Better to just keep dancing.

She took a long drag on her cigarette and tried not think about it. Bethany coming into her life had brightened it up. She'd take her under her wing and make sure the girl didn't get hurt.

There were a lot of ways a girl could get hurt. A lot of people want to hurt you, use you, abuse, you, chew you up and spit you back out and that's why a gal has to get tough, has to learn to look out for herself.

Bethany has none of that. Poor girl. She's like a little sister, a beautiful little sister who needs help. So, I've got to be there to help her.

She stretched and got up.

All right. Run a bath, go clean up, do my makeup and

go get something to eat, see what he wants from me today.

Maybe talk to Bethany again, if the girl can get free of that aunt and uncle of hers.

Suki hadn't seen her for a while.

Wonder what's going on.

They were angry she'd cut off her hair. I don't envy her, having relatives like that. Though they had money, that's for sure. That girl was kept tighter than a mummy wrapped in a tomb. No room to breathe at all.

Suki stretched arms over her head like a cat. And stretched and stretched. Dancer's muscles waking up, feeling her body.

Yeah.

No corsets for me. Just free.

A knock came on the door, and she went to answer it.

Rocco stood there, a glowering frown on his face.

Something was wrong.

"Rocco?" She stepped back, opening the door further. "Come in."

He stepped in, and she closed the door behind him. "Sit. Anywhere." She moved over to the dresser where two liquor bottles stood. "I'll pour you a drink." She reached for a bottle.

He raised his hand, palm toward her in a stop motion. "Leave it."

She set the bottle back down, as a sinking feeling filled her empty belly

Frowning, she fumbled for a cigarette, as Rocco sat down, watching her with that look on his face. The look that was making her more and more nervous.

She placed the cigarette in the long, elegant holder before lighting it. She didn't feel like sitting down. Whatever it was that had put that look on his face, she would hear it standing up.

"Police just pulled a man's body out of Lake Catherine. He was shot four times. The man was Frank."

She sank onto the corner of the bed, deflated. She stared at Rocco. "Frank? Dead? No."

It couldn't be. Frank couldn't be dead.

"He's taking me to the opera," she said. "He's going to pick up the tickets after his job is done. He promised..."

"Listen." Rocco stood and grabbed her by the arm. "There ain't time for this. So, listen up. Cops pulled his body from Lake Catherine. They'll be asking questions."

"I don't know anything," she said with a frown and a shake of her head. "I'm a clam, remember?"

Rocco nodded. "Good. You keep it that way."

"But Rocco," she looked into his eyes, pleading. "What happened to Frank? Why was he on the lake? What happened to my Frank?"

"They shot him in the back." Rocco shook his head. "Four times. He never saw it coming."

"Who?"

"You don't know from nothing." Rocco shook his head again. "And you don't need to know. Al will deal with them. Don't you worry about that, doll."

"What do I do now?"

"You keep your mouth shut," he said. "Like always."

"Tell Al not to worry about me. I'm a clam."

"He ain't worried, doll. He knows you. You'll stay here. Al will take care of everything. Arrangements for his body are to have it sent back to Chicago. Funeral a few days after. You'll ride along on the train. Make sure everything goes smooth."

"I can do that."

"Now, when the coppers come, you're just the dancer, see? Here to take the baths ,and on vacation with your boyfriend," Rocco said.

She just nodded.

He saw himself out and she reached for the bottle of rum which was almost empty again.

a girl like Bethany would never understand all this. She needs to be careful not to get sucked up in this lifestyle.

Suki poured the last of the rum into her glass.

She seems happy enough. She's a sweet girl. She'll be all right. Once she gets away from that aunt and uncle of hers.

She doesn't need to be doin' this kind of thing. Living this kind of life. I don't want her in this kind of mess I got in. I do not want her in this. She doesn't need to be doing this kind of thing, living this kind of life.

She needs to go off with that young gentleman of hers, and stay away from Al's men. She's just too sweet to be able to do well with the likes of them.

A man like that will eat her up and spit her out, why, he'd have her twisted around his finger. And some of these men ain't so nice. Ain't so nice as Frank.

"Oh, Frank, what have they done to you, what have they done to you?" She spoke to the empty room as if he were there with her. "I sorta miss ya. And, again, I sorta don't. Some of the things you done to me, why, I'd never want a girl like Bethany to go through them. Some of them things you done to me ought not to be done to any girl. I forgive you for all of them, each and every one of them. But I'm glad those things won't happen again."

She shook her head in silence now, over-whelmed by how he life had turned out, and what they had done to Frank, shooting him in the back like cowards. He was a good shooter and shouldn't have gone out that way. She couldn't help imagining it, and the image she created in her head made her sad and frightened.

Who would protect her now?

"Maybe I need to get away," she muttered. "Somewhere where they won't find me."

She stood up and started to pace in front of the window.

"Maybe I need to start again, with somethin' else. I don't know what, or where, or when. But I can't stay here. I can't stay here, livin' this life. Be a gangsters moll again. All this mess continuin'. Life is too short. We're livin' it too fast. Too damn fast. And dancing faster don't make it better, don't make it better. "

She shook her head.

"I used to think it did. But dancing too fast don't

make it better. It don't make it better. It just keeps me busy, until I start it all up again, until it all starts up again. Don't make it better. Any more than drinkin' too much bathtub gin."

She stopped and addressed the chair as if someone were sitting in it.

"The trouble is, I have had troubles with men. I have had troubles with men. Now, if I could just find me a good man, one like Bethany's, Bethany's policeman. If I could just find me a man like that, oh, I'd be so good to him; I'd be so very, very good to him. I need to find me a good man. A real good man."

She walked back to the window, and paused looking out.

"Wonder where I'll find him if I ever will. Wherever you are, you good, good man, I need to find you soon."

She emptied the last of the rum into her glass, and then sank into the chair. He head fell back against it, she drained the rum, and soon she was snoring, the empty glass falling to the floor.

BETHANY KNOCKED TWICE, before Suki opened the door.

The first knock woke her and she made herself get up, and move toward the door. She didn't know how long she'd been asleep, but she had one hell of a hangover.

She opened the door.

"Bethany."

Suki darted her gaze frantically, up and down the hall, looking to see who had seen Bethany knock on the door.

So far no one.

"Come in. Hurry."

Bethany slipped through the door, and Suki closed and locked it.

"Paul just told me the police pulled a man's body out of Lake Catherine. It was Frank. He'd been shot four times." Bethany's brows gathered with concern, and her gaze reached out to Suki. "Is it true? Is Frank really dead?"

"Yes." Suki said in a dull tone. "They shot him in the back. Rocco said he never saw it coming."

"How?"

"It's better if you don't know any more than that. He was doing something the boss sent him to do. That's all I know. Even that is too much. The police questioned me, and so did Mr. Capone."

She glanced at Bethany, her eyes bright. "It's best just to be a pretty girl, the life of the party, arm candy that lights up a room, but not so bright that you notice things. See?"

Bethany nodded.

"You remember that." Suki gave a slight frown, then looked away, at the window.

"We had plans, Frank and me." Her voice hitched. "He promised to take me to the opera. I've always wanted to see one, and he said he'd take me, once the job was done. Only, he never came back."

"Oh, Suki. I'm so sorry."

"Yeah." Ski paced to the window and reached for her flask, now that the rum bottle was empty.

Soon she'd be completely out of hootch.

"I'm sorry, too." She took a gulp of rum from the flask.

"Opera is probably overrated anyway." She turned to Bethany, holding the flask. "You want some?"

"No, thanks."

"I don't know what I'm gonna do now. I've got to find myself a new sugar daddy, and soon."

"I thought you loved Frank."

"I did, but he wasn't the love of my life, and now Frank's dead.What am I gonna to do now? A girl's gotta eat."

"Don't you have any money?"

"Not enough to last. Frank took real good care of me, but I didn't want him to leave me holding the bag. So, I didn't get involved in his business." She shrugged, and wiped the mascara from beneath her eyes with a hanky embroidered with the letter F.

She glanced at it, blinked twice, and threw it

onto the dresser. "Come on. We'll go dancing at the club."

"I don't know, Suki. Wouldn't it be better for you to stay out of sight? If the police, or whoever killed Frank, are watching you…"

"Let 'em watch. I just want to put on my glad rags, dance, and have a ball," Suki said. "Life's too damn short."

"I wish I could go dancing with you, but I've already promised Rocco I'd wait for him to call. He's taking me to dinner tonight."

"Oh, in that case, you'd better wait by the phone. Never be someplace other than where Rocco tells you to be."

Bethany frowned. "Why?"

"Oh, you're so wet behind the ears." Suki sighed. "You just do whatever Rocco tells you to do, and you'll be fine. He'll take good care of you. But never make him angry. Understand?"

Bethany nodded. "Yes."

"Good girl." Suki swept a red dress off the back of a chair, and handed it to Bethany. "Here. Wear this tonight. Red is his favorite color, and you'll want to take his mind off things, to keep him in a good mood. Whatever you do, keep him in a good mood."

"Thank you," Bethany said.

"Go on, now. You'd better be in your room, in case he calls to check on you."

"Are you going to be all right?"

"You're sweet, but you don't need to worry about me, doll. I'm like a cat. Always land on my feet. Go on, now." Suki waved her away.

Bethany nodded and slipped out the door, closing it softly behind her.

SUKI WOULD BE LEAVING the next day on the train, which would take Frank's body back to Chicago for burial.

Mr. Capone assumed she'd be the one to travel with the body, and, though he'd made all the arrangements, so she wouldn't have to, she knew he expected her to be the grieving moll, just like a widow.

In her own way, she did grieve for Frank, though she knew he wasn't the love of her life. Not her soul mate. They'd had their time together and much of it had been good and loving.

Considering the circumstances, it had been as good as it ever could have been.

They'd been thrown together, and their physical chemistry had been off the charts. Fast and intense, they were insatiable in their sexual desire for each other.

But it took more than that to be true love, the kind to last a lifetime.

Bethany had come to say goodbye to Suki before

she left, and Suki realized she might not see her young friend again.

Life was like that. You never knew who was moving into or out of your life. That's why you had to stay in the today, in the now.

She hoped Bethany was on a path to happiness, and not heartbreak. There was so much she wished she could tell her.

"You can have many loves," Suki said. "But you never love in the same way twice. Each love is as different as the one you love."

"He's my first and only love," Bethany said. "I want no other."

"You were born under a lucky star," Suki said. "I hope you'll always have your one and only love."

"I'm sorry you lost your Frank," Bethany said, tears gathering in her eyes.

"Not sure how much he was mine," Suki said. "He wasn't one to let anyone in deep. But he made sure I knew, and everyone else knew, that he considered me his. And for a while, I was." Suki changed the subject then, to avoid her mood shifting. "So, you two are taking off?"

"Yes. I have to go back and figure out my financial situation." Bethany smiled. "It's a good one, but I have to learn how to manage it. And then look into going to college, and also find a place to have our wedding. You'll come, I hope?"

"I'm so happy for you." She reached for

Bethany's hand, and squeezed it. "Of course, I'll come. Wouldn't miss it."

About an hour after Bethany left, just as Suki had almost finished packing her clothes, the phone rang.

It was Phillip. She'd called Phyllis, after getting the news about Frank, and now that Phillip was back from his business trip, he'd heard what had happened.

"My condolences on your loss," Phillip said. "How are you holding up?"

Hearing Phillip's voice on the phone made Suki want to close her eyes as she listened. It made her wish Phillip was there, as she'd realized she had no true friends back in Chicago. And she didn't really want to go back there.

Her Chicago friends were good to go out for a drink with, but that was all. Her roommate Tessa had sent her a note that had arrived yesterday which read:

I figured you weren't coming back since all your clothes and shoes are gone. If you do show up again I guess I don't owe you nothin'. I got a new man and he's goin' west so I'm goin' with him. Maybe you'll never see this, but if ya do, there's a picture of you an' me I thought you might want for old times sake. I got one for me so this one's for you.

Keep dancing doll, and don't take no guff off anyone, especially Frank.

Tessa

Suki could've disappeared in Miami, or even here in Hot Springs, and they'd never have even missed her, except for her roommate.

Maybe. She wasn't sure about Tessa.

She needed better friends, and she had them now, in Phillip and Phyllis. They truly did care.

"I did love him, and I know he loved me," she said, to answer Phillip. "But it never was Shangri-La." She sighed. "And I don't think it ever could have been. He was a dangerous man, doing a dangerous job. I think this was bound to happen, eventually. It just, well, it came as a shock, even so."

"Do you want Phyllis, or me, to come be with you?"

"No. I have to travel back to Chicago, with his body. Mr. Capone expects that, and I want to do it. But I can't stay there. So after the funeral, I'll go."

"Where will you go?"

"I don't know."

"We'd like you to come stay with us. You can be with friends ,while you decide what to do next. Rest, and grieve. Whatever you need."

"You're very kind. I think I would like that, to stay with you." She hastily added, "The two of you."

"Then do. Your room is here waiting, whenever you are ready."

"Thank you, Phillip," she said. "I appreciate it."

THE TRAIN RUMBLED ALONG, as she stared out the window. She'd stuck to her room. and her flask. Now she felt restless, and went out into the hall, to head for the dining car.

She stumbled, walking down the hall, and her flask fell out of her robes pocket, to the ground. She stared at the silver flask Frank had given her.

"Is she drunk," a woman in a full corset, and floor length dress said. "She is. She's drunk."

"Come along, Madeline," her husband said, taking her by the arm to draw her away. "I'll call for the porter."

The woman pulled her dress aside so the fabric of her dress wouldn't brush against Suki, while the woman's sneer brushed all over her.

"Upstage bluenose," Suki muttered. "Into my business. Go on, get out of here."

And then it struck her.

She'd sounded just like her mother. The mother she'd sworn never to be anything like.

She sat staring at the flask. Then she made her way to standing, by holding onto the wall, and turned and went back into her room.

When the porter knocked on her door, saying, "Miss Suki, are you all right?" She opened the door.

Thrusting the now empty flask at him, she said, "Dispose of this for me. I am done with it."

She had been on a toot long enough. She was done with a lot of things Frank had pulled her into, and drunk or not, she knew it.

The porter took the flask from her, as if it was of no consequence, something that happened every day. "Would you care for some coffee?"

"No. I'm going to sleep," she said. "A nice long sleep. Wake me 'fore we get there, 'an bring coffee then."

"Yes miss," he said with a nod, closing her door.

She didn't bother locking it, and climbed onto the bed, then kicked off her shoes, laid her head on the pillow, and closed her eyes.

Sleep was what she needed. Lots and lots of sleep.

* * *

Suki's mother, Janine Chesterfield, lived in the same small house in Chicago she'd always lived in, on the wrong side of the tracks. But this time she had a new husband, and a new ring on her finger.

Her name was now Janine Weiman, and her new husband owned a seedy bar down the street. They'd be moving into quarters over the top of it soon. Boxes filled the living room.

"So, you heard I got married again, and decided to pay me a visit," Janine said, her tone flat. Then it raised in that old accusatory high pitched tone, as her anger came out. "You just had to get into my business again, didn't you?"

The night on the train came back to Suki.

She was glad she'd gotten rid of the flask. It was too easy to drink all day long, when she carried that flask around with her. She didn't need to keep everything Frank had given her.

If she was going to make a new start some things had to go.

Suki's mother had aged since she'd seen her. Gray, stringy hair, and dull skin. Bloodshot eyes. A potbelly, like one you'd usually see on a man. The drink had been destroying her health for years, and now it was really showing.

It was hard to have sympathy for someone who so willfully destroyed their health, even if the woman was her mother. This visit would be short, and then it would be over and done.

"No," Suki said. "I had no idea you'd married again, and I've been out of town."

"Out of town?" Her mother frowned. "Where? And why?"

Now, who is all into whose business?

Suki held back her thought, as she always did around her mother.

There was no point speaking it. That would only bring on a fight.

"It doesn't matter now," Suki said. "I came back to bury a friend, and then I'm moving."

"Friend?" Her mother laughed derisively. "You mean that gangster you took up with."

"Frank Omato was my friend."

"You were his moll," her mother shook her head. "He wasn't your friend. Men can't be friends with a woman. They only want one thing."

"Tell it to Sweeny!" Suki said. "I don't buy that. What Frank and I had was different. We were friends and lovers. But I don't expect you to understand."

"You're not the kind of woman who has male friends; you're the kind who takes lovers," her mother said.

"You mean like you. You think I'm just like you. Well, I'm not."

Suki was too angry now, to keep holding back her words.

She'd sworn to herself that she'd never be like her mother, and she wasn't going to be.

"At the end of the day, you spread your legs for him, like any other woman," her mother said. "You're no different, no better than anyone else." She snarled. "He would have replaced you in an hour."

There was her mothers anger, a constant thing, the rage that Suki had grown up around. The drinking, the men, and the ugly hurtful words.

It made her want to throw up, being back in this house, listening to her mother again. And she hadn't had a single drop of alcohol all day.

Something that had been more challenging than

she'd thought it would be. It had become more of a crutch than the crutches she'd gotten rid of after her foot healed.

Coming back to the home she'd grown up with was also much harder than she'd imagined.

But having done it this time, she never had to go back. In this moment she made a large decision.

Suki was determined to change her life, now that Frank was gone, and she would start by moving to Miami after the funeral was over and done. She would go stay with Phyllis and Phillip, and get her life back on track. The decision was done.

But she wouldn't tell her mother after all. Because her mother did not care.

I don't know why I came here. Why I tried again. She never changes, and she's not going to.

"I came by to see how you were, because you're my mother," she said. "And because I love you."

Her mother just grunted.

She was never going to say the words back.

It was the last time Suki would ever say them. She didn't owe her mother a thing.

Best to keep moving on, into a better, healthier life.

"Well, hope you have a good life with the new guy," Suki said.

Her mother just looked at her.

Suki let herself out the door.

* * *

The funeral was a gray, gloomy affair, as it rained all that weekend in Chicago.

Mr. Capone and his cronies sent so many flowers the casket was surrounded by them, and the big white spray on the top had a scent that made Suki feel ill.

On top of this was the fact that she hadn't taken a drop of giggle water since she'd seen her mother.

She wanted her wits sharp. Wishing she hadn't eaten that day, she pressed an embroidered handkerchief to her mouth, and closed her eyes before opening them again.

The gang, of course, took that to mean she was grieving, and the men were very attentive to her.

As Frank had always said, they took care of their own.

Since her apartment had been rented out, and she'd gotten a room in a cheap hotel, Mr. Capone had sent Rocco, to move her to a more expensive, safer hotel, with a nice room.

Of course she knew this was mostly for show. Al wouldn't want it said that his people didn't have the best.

She also knew this treatment wasn't going to last, and she'd have to do something, or some brute of a man who worked for Al would be sniffing after her, wanting to be the next in line, after Frank.

Living with her mother, she'd learned there was always another man waiting in the wings to be the next man, in a beautiful woman's bed. And some were not so patient.

There'd been status in being Frank's moll, so there would be status in bedding his moll, and in winning her.

No, she had to get out of Chicago, to make a clean break, without her past sticking to her, to mess things up in her new life.

* * *

She moved through the funeral, and the week after in a fog, grieving Frank at times, and keeping her other thoughts to herself, as she didn't want anyone to know her plans.

The day she left town, she simply got a taxi, went to the train station, bought her ticket, and got on the next train to Miami.

If Mr. Capone wanted to find her, he would. She'd tell him the grief was too much, so she'd had to get out of Chicago.

She wouldn't tell him she'd decided to make a permanent move to Miami.

Better to apologize than to ask for permission.

If she was lucky, they would all be too busy, and with her enough out of sight and out of mind, they would eventually forget about her.

She was just another hoofer after all. They could always find a new dancer.

BEING ON THE SAME TRAIN, riding back to Miami, brought memories, though not of Frank.

Every little thing about the train reminded her of Phillip, and as the miles stretched away from Chicago, she felt as if her past was being peeled away, releasing her like those Florida orange peels released the tasty fruit within.

She couldn't wait to get her hands on a fresh Florida orange, and she couldn't wait to get on with her new life.

The train couldn't move fast enough for her, as she made lists in her head, of all the things she wanted to taste, to see, and to do.

This time she was going to ride that elephant.

She was going dancing in the club with Phyllis.

She was going to say yes to going out with Phillip, when he asked her.

Soon she would see Phillip again.

With each thought and each mile she came more and more alive. Back to herself.

Suki looked out the window, as the train pulled to a stop at the station in Miami.

She saw him just as the train stopped.

Phillip.

He was there waiting for her, watching.

She'd never been so glad to see anyone in her life.

Gathering her things, she hurried to disembark. She stepped out into the warm Florida air, and there he was.

Barely had she stepped off the train, when her first urge was to run to him. So she ran.

He pulled her into his arms, and held her close, his hand rubbing her back.

The comfort of his hand upon her back spread through her.

It was as if he knew just what she needed.

Strong, warm, and protective, his arms held her.

She felt as if she'd come home.

She was free, and she was home here. Leaving the last time had been a mistake. She'd known it deep down in her heart when she'd left; despite the logical reasons she'd had for going, her heart had said stay.

This was where she belonged, and she never wanted to go away again.

"I'm glad you came back," Philip said. "I missed you."

"I missed you too," she said. "Ever so much."

They drew apart again.

He stood looking down at her. "Your room is ready. Phyllis insisted on redecorating it."

"Oh my goodness. She didn't have to do that." She shook her head.

"Well, you know Phyllis," he said with a grin.

"Yes," she smiled. "She loves to decorate."

"We both want you to feel at home," he said. "And I hope you will consider our home, your home."

"Thank you," she said. "You're the best kind of friend."

But they were more than friends. Could be more than friends now. Any danger to her was now gone.

His lips descended in a gentle kiss, which touched hers, before she fully got the last word out, and she gave herself up to the kiss.

The warmth of this lips, the way he tasted, the gentle kiss drew her spirit up and up, until she might have floated into the clouds. She forgot every word, every thought. There was only this kiss, soul-to-soul, as if meeting for the first time kind of kiss.

It is said the first kiss sets the tone for the relationship, and this kiss, a meeting of two souls, meant to be together, forever was a kiss beyond compare.

He drew away slow, then, his eyes holding all the love and kindness he had inside, gazed into hers, as he said, "I couldn't wait one moment longer. I want to be more than just your friend. I intend to woo you, and win you. I want to get to know you better. I want you to know me. So I will give you time to grieve, and to learn what you want. But you must know, I want more of these kisses."

"I want more too," she whispered.

This seemed like a dream, too good to be true. It was all she'd dreamed of, and more.

"Phillip, what does cuidado mi Amor mean? You said it to me that night on the train, long ago," she said.

"It means careful sweetheart, or careful beloved," he said, smiling at her, the words soft from his lips.

Lips she watched, as she wanted him to kiss her again.

She gasped and her fingers flew to her lips. "Beloved?"

"Yes," he nodded.

"Kiss me again, please," she said. "I want more of these kisses. Lot's more. That kiss made my heart dance."

"Then let us dance again, upon the clouds, with a kiss, Mi Amor." He smiled. And then he bent to kiss her again.

THE END

TRAPPING THE BUTTERFLY: CHAPTER ONE

*B*ethany Robinson did not need yet another lecture on being appreciative.

"Thank you, Aunt Margaret."

She accepted the gold trimmed, white china plate her aunt handed her, while clearing her throat to disguise the grumbling of her stomach. Placing the plate in front of her on the table, she waited and tried not to look at the food placed upon it.

At the head of the table, Uncle James cut a big bite of chicken and popped it into his mouth without waiting for anyone.

Aunt Margaret said nothing, but straightened her fork with that look upon her face, her lips puckering like a prune. She straightened the fork again, showing her blue veins and the bones beneath her thin, pale skin.

Aunt Margaret was in a mood, and she obviously wasn't going to say Grace.

So it would be one of *those* kinds of meals.

If only Bethany could have eaten in the kitchen, with cook as she'd been allowed to when she was younger.

She glanced down at her chicken, wondering if it was safe to eat a bite or if that would draw her aunt's attention and sour mood.

Perhaps it would be best to wait.

The tension in the room gathered closer, and the more she could distance herself from that, the better.

Her stomach rumbled again.

"Margaret," Uncle James said. "Please eat something."

Her aunt, a small, bird-like woman, who barely ate enough to keep a bird alive, said, "I couldn't eat another bite."

Such a predictable old refrain.

"Not a thing." Aunt Margaret sighed. "You go on, dear. Take it."

She held out her plate to him, looking away from it as if the food offended her. "I simply can't."

Bethany would have loved for her aunt to have offered *her* the savory chicken she had passed over to Uncle James, but she said nothing and instead cut her own portion into small pieces and ate one slow bite so as not to draw attention to herself.

Having an entire breast of chicken all for herself

just once would be nice. Her aunt always cut the chicken breasts in half.

One might fill her up. *If anything could.*

Bethany suspected Aunt Margaret counted how many bites Bethany took. Though counting bites was something Bethany did, too, it was different when she did it.

Four more bites, see? Out of five. If she chewed them slowly enough, she might feel full faster. *Strange how that sometimes worked. That, and drinking lots of water.*

Though not today. Not the way Aunt Margaret stared at her with that look, her brown eyes darkening like storm clouds gathering.

Thump.

"Enough!" Uncle James thumped his fist on the table again, his fork still in his hand.

Both women turned to him in surprise.

"Enough. I'm taking you to Hot Springs National Park for the baths, and you will not argue with me."

Bethany raised one eyebrow. He wasn't talking to her. She never argued with Uncle James. *What was he talking about? What did he mean by enough?*

"One likes to be asked." Aunt Margaret sniffed and her facial expression turned haughty. "There is no need to speak to a lady in that tone, Mr. Robinson."

"Mrs. Robinson, I am asking you to travel with me to the medicinal springs to partake of the baths and healing proper- ties of the waters." His tone brooked no argument and said just as clearly that he was not asking, but telling.

"I will think about it."

Uncle James, knowing as well as Bethany did, that the phrase Aunt Margaret had just used meant *no,* then changed both his tone and his approach. "I am asking out of concern for you, dear. Your health is no better and seems to be getting worse."

"I have done everything the doctor asked."

"Yes, and now we are going to try a new doctor. One who has had success with women in your condition."

What exactly was that condition? They always referred to it as *one of Aunt Margaret's spells.* Maybe this new doctor would finally have a name for it.

"The trip will do you good, and I have a meeting with Mr. Rivalde after we arrive."

"About the merger we've been discussing?" She glanced over at Bethany then back again.

"Yes. He is amiable."

"Well, then." Aunt Margaret sniffed. "We shall all go to Hot Springs and take the baths." She shot a pointed glance at Bethany.

Bethany placed her hands in her lap and folded her fingers together. "When are we going?"

"Next week," Uncle James said. "We'll take a two week holiday." He nodded at his wife again. "That should be long enough."

Aunt Margaret nodded in agreement.

Would two weeks be long enough to cure her aunt? *That didn't seem like very long.*

Oh, but if we're gone that long...

"That means we'll be away on my birthday," Bethany blurted out, and then stopped herself from saying more.

This would be her eighteenth birthday. She'd moved from counting down the months to counting the weeks left. Soon she would be of age and no longer under Aunt Margaret's thumb.

"We'll celebrate your birthday in Hot Springs. That will make it a very memorable trip." Aunt Margaret smiled a secretive smile.

That smile would have made Bethany nervous had they *not*

been discussing her birthday.

Just a week left to plan before they left for Hot Springs, Arkansas.

Bethany would have to change her original idea, but she would still go through with it. Nothing short of illness or death would stop her from carrying out her plan.

Being in Hot Springs might even make it easier.

* * *

Bethany had never been inside the train station before. She peered out beneath her wide brimmed hat as she looked about taking in the sights and sounds around her.

Her aunt resembled a crow in a tailored black worsted jersey suit, gray hat, and black shoes as she darted her gaze about the station, looking for an open space on one of the wooden benches.

Not for the first time, Bethany noticed how old fashioned her aunt appeared in the skirt that came nearly to her ankles. The suit was at least five years old, and her aunt wouldn't re- place it until it wore out. Despite the fact Mr. Robinson owned his own company and moved among the wealthier members of society, his frugal wife stretched every penny and clung to the older fashions.

Most of the women bustling about the station wore newer fashions and shorter skirts. Bethany glanced down at her own navy blue georgette crepe frock which fell well below the knee, the long, lacy collar the only pretty thing she liked about it. At least with her wide brimmed hat, she could duck her head and hide when she wanted to.

Oh, what she wouldn't give to wear one of those shorter dropped waist dresses with a cloche hat and bobbed hair. To look like other girls her age and to go dancing with boys. She could not wait for the day when she could pick out her own clothes and go when and where she wanted. Soon she would be eighteen and would be able to use her inheritance. She hoped. Uncle James had always been vague about the terms of the will and monies her parents had left behind for her.

"Come along," Aunt Margaret said, interrupting her thoughts. "We will sit and wait for your uncle."

"Yes, ma'am."

Bethany followed her aunt, who had noticed an open spot on one of the benches and strode toward it determined to claim it for her own. People moved away from her when she was in that mood and held that look upon her face. Her aunt, tiny as she was, could be a formidable woman. Soon she and Bethany sat together on a high backed wooden bench.

People bustled around the train station, many carrying newspapers and reading the headlines as they walked.

Everyone else appeared to be reading the paper. *Something must have happened.*

A long line of passengers stretched around the newspaper stand, and more joined the line as soon as it started to shorten.

Whatever had happened must have been awful. Women cried, and men shook their heads and looked mournful.

Bethany strained to see a newspaper held by a man nearby. The headline read, *Rudolph Valentino Dead, August 23, 1926 Sudden Death at the Age of Thirty-One.*

Oh, no. He couldn't be dead. He'd just had an opera-

tion a week ago. His latest movie had just come out, and he'd gone to New York to promote it. He was too young to be dead. So young and handsome. How could Rudolph Valentino be dead?

A tear formed in the corner of Bethany's eye. Uncle James sat down next to her, and she asked, "Uncle James, are you gonna buy a newspaper?"

"What for?" He frowned. Uncle James read the business news and kept up daily with Wall Street, but rarely followed stories unless they were about money or politics.

"To read about what happened to Rudolph Valentino."

"You want to read about the death of some movie star?" Uncle James directed his frown at her.

"Well, yes. Everyone is mourning him. Can't you see?"

"He must have been a drinker," Aunt Margaret said.

"That's what happens to wild young men who drink."

"Hollywood types," Uncle James said with disdain. "They all drink."

"The women, too. It's disgraceful. "Aunt Margaret nodded.

Both she and Uncle James were in favor of prohibition and looked down on lawbreakers. Aunt Margaret always pointed out how all the good churches now served grape juice in place of communion wine.

"Well, there's nothing in that paper I wish to read." Uncle James pulled out his pocket watch to look at it, signaling the discussion was closed.

"Young women today..." Aunt Margaret paused and let the words trail away. "I simply don't understand them."

The dark haired flapper who had drawn Aunt Margaret's attention walked by, cigarette holder in hand, as if on cue to emphasize Aunt Margaret's point.

"Drinking, smoking, running wild." Aunt Margaret tisked and then sniffed and turned her head away from the flapper, dis- missing the thin, vivacious girl who was now talking with friends.

Ignoring Aunt Margaret, Bethany fingered her clutch purse. She'd saved for months to collect the money inside it. Though she yearned for a newspaper, she knew that if she bought one, it meant dipping into her funds.

Best not to dip into it for anything, or her plan might fail.

"I blame the parents," Aunt Margaret said. "You are a fortunate young lady. Why if we hadn't taken you in? Who knows what might have happened to you?"

"Yes, ma'am. Thank you." The words slipped out

automatically, the pattern long established from ten years of similar conversations.

Bethany looked about the room, taking in that her aunt and uncle seemed to be the only people in the train station un- interested in the death of Rudolph Valentino.

Was the whole world mourning his death? Everyone, except perhaps Aunt Margaret and Uncle James.

At least here, Bethany didn't feel so all alone, as if no one understood her or her feelings. As if no one felt the way she did, and that she had something wrong with her.

Here, she felt more normal.

Maybe someone would leave a newspaper when they were done, and she could pick it up and read their copy.

Unfortunately, the train arrived before that happened, and the conductor called all aboard.

A movie poster beside the door where they went out to board the train advertised Valentino's final movie. It read, *Rudolph Valentino stars with Vilma Banky in The Son of the Sheikh, from the novel by E.M. Hull.*

How romantic. What an adventure a trip to a foreign land would be. To have a Sheik fall in love with you and sweep you away.

Bethany sighed.

Oh, how she wanted to see the movie. Everyone had been talking about it since it had premiered in

California in July. Then the promotional tour had taken the stars across the county-

try, and Rudolph Valentino had ended up in New York having his operation. Now, he was dead.

Bethany might never have a chance to see one of his movies.

She sat on the train in their private compartment in the window seat looking out at the world and wondering when, where, and how she would ever find her place in it. Someplace where she fit in, and where at least one person understood her. She wanted to see *The Son of the Sheikh* so badly. The movie was supposed to open next week at home. Any day now, and everyone would see it but her.

Once again, she would miss out. She missed out on every- thing.

She stared out the window at the scenery. The whole world was passing her by, and right now she was powerless to do any- thing about it.

They rode the Rock Island Railroad into Hot Springs, Arkansas, and then took a taxi to the Arlington Hotel. With two towers on top and an American flag flying in the middle, the hotel sat at the end of famous Bathhouse Row and soared impressively over all the other buildings. Bethany counted at least nine floors with windows, not counting the towers.

Their taxi let them off out front, and the taxi driver un- loaded their bags for the bellman to take in. Uncle James walked up to the reception desk to check them in while Bethany waited with Aunt Margaret.

"It's beautiful," Bethany said. Inside the Lobby, two murals adorned the walls: one behind the bar on the right side of the room, and the other behind the bandstand on the left side.

Her aunt glanced about, sniffed, and said, "I hope our rooms are suitable. One never knows with a hotel."

Bethany had no frame of reference with which to compare this hotel, since she'd never been inside one before, so she remained silent and enjoyed all the new sights and sounds.

Once they finished checking in, they followed the bellman to the elevator and then accompanied him up to their rooms on the fifth floor, where he unlocked both doors. They stepped inside, and he placed their bags in their respective rooms.

Bethany hurried to the window in her room and looked out. She had an excellent view of Bathhouse Row and was high enough up to see quite far. The room was small but lovely, and she had it all to herself. Though her aunt and uncle would be right next-door, she was happy to have the privacy. She'd be able to lock the door so no one could walk in on her, not even her aunt.

"You have an hour to unpack and freshen up,

and then we'll go down to the Venetian Dining Room for dinner," Uncle James said. "Be ready."

"Yes, sir." Bethany waited until he left before spinning in a circle with her arms out and laughing. She was here inside this elegant room in Hot Springs, where her life would change for- ever. She could hardly wait.

* * *

Trapping the Butterfly, book one
Debra Parmley's Butterflies Fly Free series

EXOTIC BUTTERFLY: CHAPTER ONE EXCERPT

*P*hyllis Garcia, filled with excitement for her journey and the chance to live in a new country, hurried over to the side of the ocean liner to gaze out upon the Puerto de Sevilla, and down at the people below.

The urge to untie her hat and remove it to feel the ocean breeze was strong, but too many eyes were watching her, expecting her to behave like the lady she'd been raised to be.

Dolores, her lady's maid, who stood next to her said, "It's so exciting!"

"Yes!" Phyllis smiled wide. "What a grand adventure this will be."

A crewman had directed them to a good spot by the rails as the ship readied to sail away from Spain to the United States of America.

It could not be soon enough for Phyllis.

Had her mother still been living, the journey would have been made much more difficult, if not impossible.

But Mrs. Garcia had passed three years ago. Once the estate was settled, Phyllis's twin brother, Phillip, had sailed to Miami, Florida, and set up a new branch of the family shipping company.

Now Phyllis was going there to join him.

While their family had diminished in numbers, the family fortunes had not.

Everything Phillip touched flourished, and their older cousin, Vicente still lived in Sevilla and managed the family interests there with great success.

Phyllis would have been expected to remain in Seville all her life and to marry well, after a long formal engagement. To do as her mother and grand-mother had done.

But that was not what Phyllis wanted.

Juana stood on the pier, waving to Phyllis, and dabbing at her eyes with her embroidered hand-kerchief.

"Dear Juana," Phyllis said to Dolores as she waved back to Juana. "She will likely stand and wave until the ship is a spec on the horizon."

Dolores nodded. "Maybe longer."

Juana had been her mother's lady's maid and had helped her mother chose a lady's maid who would help to guide her daughter to fill a proper place in the society in which they lived.

Benita was older and stricter than Juana.

From the day they had first met, Phyllis could not abide her.

Her initial reaction had proved correct.

Benita always pulled the corset strings too tight and would fix Phyllis's long black hair in such tight settings that Phyllis frequently came down with headaches.

Everyone thought her delicate, and such a lady, when she retired to her room to rest and hopefully be rid of the pain in her head.

They had no idea that the first thing she would do, inside her room, was pull out all the hairpins, and let the heavy tresses fall, down past her shoulders.

Soon that would all be in the past. She hoped to never have headaches like that again.

"Did you pack scissors?" she asked Dolores.

"Yes," Dolores nodded. "I have everything on the list that you wanted."

"Excellent," Phyllis said.

Her transformation would go as planned. She would leave the corsets and her long hair behind.

When she disembarked from the ship in the United States, she would emerge as a modern woman.

Like the flappers in the magazines.

The magazines weren't something she could run out and buy, so her brother sent them to her, along with other things her mother would have found shocking.

Juana would have been horrified at what Phyllis planned to do.

But she wouldn't know.

The transformation would take place right before the ship reached the U.S.

In the meantime, she had dinners onboard to attend and steamer trunks full of clothing.

Everything needed for a transformation was hidden with maids clothing in the steamer trunk she'd gifted to Dolores to pack her things.

One of the first things Phyllis had done after her mother passed was to let Benita go.

They did not need to employ two ladies' maids in the house.

Phyllis wouldn't have dreamed of letting go of the woman who had been so devoted to her mother. So dear Juana had stepped into Benita's place. Phyllis was relieved to discover her corset would not be nearly so tight, nor had Juanita ever jabbed hair-pins into Phyllis's scalp.

Things had continued as usual at the house, until Phyllis, encouraged by her brother to join him in Miami, had agreed to.

For dear Juana, there was no question of her traveling with Phyllis, or continuing as lady's maid.

She had a husband, a son, and now a new grand-daughter in Seville, where she was born and raised. She would not think of leaving them.

Phyllis and Phillip rewarded her well for her years of service and now that she had packed all the things Phyllis would take with her, and seen her off at the pier, she was officially retired and could now enjoy her grandchild.

This did not make the parting any less emotional for Juana.

She had held Phyllis after she was born and seen her mother through a difficult labor and childbirth, of not just one child, but twins.

To dear Juana, today it was as if she were losing a child.

"It is hard for her," Dolores noted.

"Yes," Phyllis said. She understood, but she was no longer a child, and she had a life to live. "But she has her new grandchild to take care of now, and that will help."

The elation Phyllis felt in escaping her expected life, for one of freedom, was too great to allow for any sadness.

"Things could not continue the way they were," she said. "Change will come, even to Spain, but it is slow because the older ones do not want change. But we cannot wait on them."

"No," Dolores agreed. "We can't."

Close in age, the two women agreed about a lot

of things. The need for women to be able to vote, to be able to drive, to be able to do so many things' men took for granted. In short, they both believed in equality for women.

Phyllis had made sure to hire a younger lady's maid who agreed about such things and felt this would be an opportunity for Dolores as well.

If she decided that wanted to do something other than being a lady's maid, Phyllis would help her.

Taking the deepest breath, she could, again she longed to be free of the corset which bound her as tightly as the expectations the old Spanish society had.

She was always expected to move within the higher levels of society, and to follow the old traditional ways of her mother and grandmother before her.

It felt as if the old ways were following her as her breath was still restricted by her clothing.

What would it feel like to be free of the horrible thing forever? To be fully free, in every way?

She didn't know but was ready to find out.

Sailing already had her feeling exhilarated, full of life, and ready for the new adventure.

She thought about all the new things she had to look forward to.

Philip said the potential for growth in Miami was unlimited. He would not be moving back.

And now, neither would she. Instead, she would

be helping him to set up their home in Miami. He'd asked her to join him to help set up the palatial home he had built and planned for them to live in.

She would be buying furnishings, decorating the grand house, so he could entertain there.

In his last letter he'd said the stables were finished. They would soon have racehorses.

There should also be gardens with rose bushes.

The thought made her think of her mother and her grandmother's rose garden.

That was one way she could honor her mother and grandmother. There were some traditions that she would continue. This one would not curtail her freedom.

I will plant a rose garden.

***

NOTE FROM THE AUTHOR

Thank you for taking the time to read *Dancing Butterfly*. If you enjoyed the story, please consider telling your friends and/or posting a review. Word of mouth is an author's best friend and much appreciated.

Dancing Butterfly, book two is Suki's story. If you have not read book one yet, *Trapping the Butterfly*, is Bethany's story. I've included chapter one as a sample chapter at the end of this book for you to enjoy.

Each story in the Butterflies Fly Free series, is about a different flapper.

In book three, *Exotic Butterfly*, you will learn more about Phylis and her twin brother Phillip with his new girlfriend, Suki. I have included a short excerpt from book three.

For fun, check out this short narration from a

section of *Dancing Butterfly* from narrator Matt Haynes:

https://www.youtube.com/watch?v=id9aEHZS b2w&list=PLBAV62yjY3lO8HMhMyyYT2SEAm4x_s KOU&index=3

And thank you for reading and reviewing! - Debra Parmley

ACKNOWLEDGMENTS

My thanks and appreciation to Michael Jack for information on trains and train routes in the 1920's; to Charles "Tazz" Welshans and to Robert Arrow for information on guns of the 1920's and for help with the gunfight scene and the train fight scene; to The Gangster Museum of Hot Springs, AR for the tour and for allowing me to hold a Thompson Submachine gun aka a "Tommy gun"; and to the staff of The Arlington Hotel.

Special thanks to my husband, for putting up with me writing all hours of the night, sometimes until the sun comes up, and for taking me to Hot Springs, Arkansas, and to The Miami Jockey Club in Miami, Florida, on our anniversary trips. Thanks to my cover artist, Sheri L. McGathy for the beautiful covers in this series; thank you to my best friend, Susan Boles and to my sister, Kimberly Lear for your support through the years.

ABOUT THE AUTHOR

Author Debra Parmley believes "Every day we are alive is a beautiful day," and she likes to give her readers and her story people a story that ends happily.

An Air Force veteran's wife, Debra writes suspense, military romantic suspense, contemporary romance, historical romance, urban fantasy romance, fairy tale romance, holiday romance, poetry, and memoir.

Debra married her high school sweetheart, whom she asked out after a five-dollar bet. After living in five states with her husband and their two sons, and then living 23 years just outside Memphis, TN, she and her husband sold everything in 2020 and now live and travel the U.S. in their 43-foot motorhome.

Debra is an adventurous writer who has worked as an independent travel agent and set foot in more than 13 countries. She has walked the plank of a pirate ship off the coast of Grand Cayman, and has gone swimming with dolphins in Moorea, French

Polynesia. She once escorted a bus full of people through Scotland.

She climbs lighthouses because she is afraid of heights.

You can see read about her travels on her Beautiful Day Traveler blog. https://beautifuldaytraveler.wordpress.com/

As Debra Bishop, she writes fairy tales for all ages, fantasy, and children's books.

Visit www.debraparmley.com

ALSO BY DEBRA PARMLEY

MILITARY ROMANTIC SUSPENSE:

Green Brotherhood SEAL Team XII series:

Finding Bryce, book one - eBook, paperback

Real Movie Hero, book two - eBook, paperback

Saving the Bellydancer, book three - eBook, paperback

Green Brotherhood Trilogy #1 - eBook boxset

Brotherhood Protectors series:

Montana Marine - book one - eBook, paperback

Defensive Instructor - book two -eBook, paperback

Marine Protector - book three- eBook, paperback

Marine Protectors - box set - eBook.

Blind Trust - book four - eBook, paperback

A Triple C Ranch Christmas Wedding - book five - eBook, paperback

Montana Delta Rescue - book six - eBook, paperback

Montana SEAL Protector - book seven - eBook, paperback

Montana Rodeo Protector - book eight - eBook,

paperback – 2024

Montana White Horse Wedding – book nine eBook, paperback - 2024

≈

Bobbins Sisters Trilogy:

Check Out – book one, eBook, paperback, audiobook.

Check In – book two, eBook, paperback.

Check Mate – book three - 2024.

≈

Single Title:

Aboard the Wishing Star - eBook, paperback, audiobook

≈

SUSPENSE -THRILLER – with Romance:

To Catch an Elf – eBook, paperback, Large Print Hardcover

≈

URBAN FANTASY ROMANCE:

Vague Directions – 2024

~

WESTERN HISTORICAL ROMANCE:

Gone to Texas: A Desperate Journey - (original sweeter version) - Large Print Hardcover, eBook, paperback.

Dangerous Ties - eBook, paperback, audiobook

Deadly Adversaries - eBook, paperback

Desperate, Dangerous, Deadly: A Western Collection – eBook box set

Isabella, Bride of Ohio: American Mail Order Bride – (original sweeter version) - Large Print Hardcover, eBook, paperback

Penny From Deadwood - coming 2024

1920's ROMANCE:

Butterflies Fly Free series:

Trapping the Butterfly – book one, eBook, paperback, audiobook, Large Print Hardcover

Dancing Butterfly – book two, eBook, paperback

Exotic Butterfly – book three, 2024

～

HOLIDAY ROMANCE:

Jenna's Christmas Wish – eBook, paperback

The Twelve Stitches of Christmas – (short story – fairy tale) – eBook

～

DYSTOPIAN ROMANCE:

The Hunger Roads Trilogy:

Another Change of Scenery – 2024

Down a Back Road – 2024

Into the Convergence Zone – 2024

～

NONFICTION:

Anywhere But Here: Our First Year Full Time RV Living on the Road – 2024

～

POETRY:

Anthology: Twilight Dips – eBook, print

Out of Print:

Protecting Pippa

Split Screen Scream

Protecting Zarifah

Vague Directions – short story

A Desperate Journey

Isabella, Bride of Ohio

Tales of Deadwood - anthology

We Know the Truth, Do You? Area 51 – anthology (going to the moon/time capsule)

Wounded Heroes - anthology

Hansel & Gretel: Down the Rabbit Hole – anthology

More Monsters from Memphis – anthology

WRITING AS DEBRA BISHOP:

Fairytales for all ages:

The Sweetest Day - Hansel and Gretel fairytale - eBook,
paperback

Fantasy:

The Rolling House – time travel serial fiction – ongoing
story.

Gatalop – 2024

Bellserie – 2024

Children's: coming in 2024.